Murder, Magic, and Maple Fudge

Sweet Spells Mysteries Book #1

A. F. Stewart

Murder, Magic, and Maple Fudge
Sweet Spells Mysteries Book #1

A. F. Stewart
Copyright © 2025 by A. F. Stewart.
All rights reserved.

Editing by Partners in Crime Book Services
Cover design by A. F. Stewart
Original artwork fully licensed by Shutterstock

Dedication

The book exists because my capricious muse got drunk and made me write a paranormal cozy mystery.

I'd also like to thank my beta readers who helped shape my ideas into a better book.

Contents

Chapter 1: The Bakery

The bakery opened in five minutes, half-a-dozen things needed finishing, and of course my employees were late on a morning when everything went wrong. I misplaced the pecans and wasted half an hour searching for them, almost burned a batch of cupcakes, and I was fairly sure I had flour smudged over my nose. Normally I could handle minor chaos, but after last night… It was enough to make me want to resort to a magic spell to speed things up.

Take a breath. You can do this.

I wiped down the counters, appreciating the smooth feel of the cloth gliding over granite and the faint scent of disinfectant. As always, the repetitive action and the cozy ambiance calmed me, and I inhaled the mix of yeasty, sugary sweet air with a hint of maple, and the smell of coffee from the percolators. Despite the time crunch, I closed my eyes and took a moment to relax.

Why did my mother have to call? Why do I let her get under my skin?

It was always the same old refrain from her. *Come home to Toronto. You belong with the coven.* Never, *how are you doing,* only listing the ways I disappointed her. She didn't understand how much I loved this place.

Moving to Easthaven Bay had been the best thing I had ever done; I was entering my thirties finally content. Since setting up shop, the Sweet Spells Bakery had become *the* place for a morning coffee and pastry. Of course, it didn't hurt that this town seemed to be the only place in Nova Scotia without a Tim Horton's coffee shop.

Yet Mother wants me to leave.

I sighed and opened my eyes, rubbing at an itch. Then promptly knocked against the sugar bowl and nearly spilled out the packets.

Yeah, things are great except when the morning goes wrong.

With a final wipe of the counter, I lined up the coffee cups, suppressing another urge to use magic to hurry things along.

Then I chuckled. My mother would disapprove of that. Maybe I should, for spite.

No. No point in courting trouble. What if someone walked in?

In the middle of arranging the maple season specials, and as if to prove me right, the bell above the door rang and footsteps echoed in the shop. I added the last fresh maple doughnut on the tray before turning around with the treats. My stomach dropped when I saw him.

Jack MacNeil.

Is the universe conspiring to ruin my morning?

Why did he have to be my first customer? A frustrating, slightly chauvinistic but gorgeous man. His blue eyes were dangerous and his smile was downright lethal, all wrapped in a smooth confidence. Being around him flustered me, exasperated me, and somehow it all translated into my acting like a twisted romantic idiot.

"Hi, Bridget." He unzipped his jacket, showing off his snug t-shirt. A whiff of his cologne drifted over the counter.

I swallowed, my mouth suddenly dry. I wanted to flee into the kitchen, but I slid the tray of doughnuts into the display case.

Calm down. He's just another customer.

Despite my racing heart and churning stomach, I asked, "What can I get you today?"

"Those maple doughnuts look good. I'll have one of them and a medium double-double coffee."

"Coming right up."

Stay cool, stay professional.

Then he added, "Oh, and you have some flour on your nose."

My anxiety soured into embarrassment, and I turned away, rubbing at my nose. Grabbing the coffee pot, I poured him a cup, thankful for the moment to collect my thoughts, adding his usual two creams and two sugars. I plated the doughnut on a paper doily and rang up his order, hoping he'd slink to a table by the window and I could ignore him.

"That will be $4.90, please."

He paid, but lingered at the counter, the steam of the coffee wisping upward between us.

"So." He smiled again with his charming, goofy grin, and ran his fingers through his wavy, light brown hair; the colour reminded me of caramel. For a second my heart fluttered like a silly schoolgirl with a crush.

Why does he have to be so handsome?

Jack shuffled his feet, rubbing his arm and rustling the nylon fabric of his jacket. "I was wondering, the church community supper on Saturday. Are—"

The bell above the door chimed again and my landlord, Jeffery Johnson, lumbered into the shop, scratching at the unkempt stubble of his face. His pot belly pushed against the fastenings of a misbuttoned flannel shirt, and a smelly, lit cigar dangled from his mouth. I scowled at him, forgetting all about Jack.

"How many times do I have to tell you, no smoking in the bakery."

Johnson scowled back at me. "Sure, sure. Hang on a sec." He waddled outside and I watched him stomp the offending smoke into the ground, before returning. I made a mental note to clean the mess up after he left.

Shuffling to the counter, Johnson edged Jack out of his way and slammed his two pudgy hands on the granite. Jack's coffee sloshed but didn't spill, and he grabbed his order, moving off to a table.

"I got your message. What do you want this time?"

I gaped, my irritation growing by the minute. "I left you that message five days ago! The washroom plumbing was backed up. Again! I had to get the plumber in and pay for it myself. You owe me for the repairs."

"I'm not paying for that! Not my fault you were impatient and didn't wait until I got to it. Tough luck on your part, I say."

"I didn't have a choice! It was violating health codes. I can't run a business with you putting off necessary repairs. You're not living up to your obligations and I'm sick of it!"

"Well, leave then. If you don't like how I run things, pack up and find a new space."

"This again? I don't know why you don't want me as your tenant anymore, but I'm not going anywhere. Except maybe to my lawyer to force you to honour our lease and do your job!"

"Screw you, lady! I'm tired of your complaints. This is broken, that is broken. This place was fine before you moved in. Now everything's wrong. I ought to kick you out on your pretty little backside. The blazes with the lease."

"You just try it, you—"

"Hey!"

We both turned to see Jack on his feet, arms crossed.

"I came here for coffee, not a fight." He looked at us like he was an elementary teacher and we were naughty children. "Take this somewhere private or cool it."

I glared, angry at his intervention and self-conscious he witnessed the argument, but before I spewed the retort waiting on my tongue, Johnson snapped at Jack.

"Stay out of this. It's none of your business."

"I disagree. When you come into a public place and disturb my meal, I'll make it my business."

Johnson stepped closer to Jack. "Well, that's you all right, MacNeil. Sticking your nose where it doesn't belong, stirring things up. Little Miss Priss over there isn't the only one I have a problem with. Just like the rest of your family, all high and mighty, thinking you're in charge. One day you'll get yours, be sure of that."

"You're welcome to try." Jack curled his hands into fists, and for a moment I thought he'd hit my landlord. The simmering confrontation shook me out of my own anger.

What is going on here?

Before anything could escalate, the bell above the door chimed for a third time, and in walked three women: Jillian Burke, Sarah Clarke and Emily Acker. I cringed. All ladies from my local coven, and while I liked Sarah, Emily was too political for me, and Jillian…well, she was a new addition to town, a stuck-up rich witch with control issues. All couture clothes and dyed, platinum blonde hair, with a superior, know-it-all attitude. And most annoying, I was her latest pet project.

I can't catch a break with customers today.

Still, I had to be polite. "Hello, ladies. What can I get you today?"

Both Jack and Mr. Johnson turned as I spoke, and Johnson looked like he'd seen a ghost.

"What are you doing here?" The words came out as a near snarl.

Emily and Sarah stared, shocked at his rude response, but Jillian sniped back, cool and dismissive.

"None of *your* business."

Johnson flushed and stepped towards the ladies.

I had enough. "Hey!" I raised my voice, startling everyone. "This is a place of business. Get out of my shop, Mr. Johnson, and stop arguing with my customers. I'll deal with you later."

My landlord glowered but backed away. "Looking forward to it." He glanced at Jack and then the women. "You'll get yours, too." Then he stalked out.

"What was that about?"

The ladies looked confused, and Jack frowned at me, then shrugged.

"Johnson's never been known for his manners. Bad disposition and worse behaviour. You know how he gets." He laughed it off with a weak chuckle and returned to his table to sip his coffee.

I gave my attention to the women. "Sorry about that. What can I get you today?"

Speaking for all, Jillian replied, "Three coffees, black. And three lightly toasted whole wheat bagels, with a scraping of butter, no cream cheese."

Emily immediately frowned. "I want cream and sugar in my coffee. And *lots* of butter, with cream cheese too."

"Nonsense." Jillian waved her hand. "You must watch your figure. Nothing fattening. Ignore those ridiculous requests, Bridget."

Emily ducked her head, arms folding in around her body. I gritted my teeth. I knew Emily was self-conscious about her weight, and Jillian hit her point-blank with it.

I wanted to smack Jillian, but I only nodded.

"Coming right up."

I rung up the order while Jillian closely watched my actions, drumming her flawlessly manicured fingers on the counter. Then she tapped her platinum card for the payment, commenting, "I hope the food lives up to the price."

Clenching my teeth, I ignored her rudeness, replying, "I'm a bit short-staffed at the moment. Why don't you sit down and I'll bring over the food when it's ready."

Jillian huffed, replying, "Don't take too long," and ushered the women to a table of her choosing, arranging their seating. She dusted off her chair before sitting and kept casting glances at me.

After a few minutes of preparation, I served them, carefully passing everyone their order, watching Emily. A smile blossomed on her face as she realized I had added sugar to her coffee and generously buttered her bagel. Screw Jillian and her manipulative ways.

After serving the ladies, I wiped down the counter and busied myself setting out more fresh pastries in the display case, trying to relax. Johnson's behaviour and Jack's presence kept nudging at my thoughts.

Why did Mr. Johnson seem shocked when the ladies walked in?

That made no sense. They all barely knew each other. Maybe Johnson was in a confrontational mood? He certainly didn't mind fighting with me, then Jack after he tried to intervene.

Why did Jack step into the argument like that? I don't need a guardian. I could have handled it.

I grinned. I could have more than handled it. Bullies like Johnson are all the same. Maybe a bad luck spell would fix him and keep him out of my hair. That would be fun. I tucked the idea into the list of possibilities.

Johnson deserves a little bad luck. A taste of his own medicine.

The neglect of his landlord duties gave me plenty of headaches. Funny, though, he had only been slacking off for a month or two. Like he was avoiding me or something. And of course, it all coincided with a rash of things going wrong in the shop. Loose tiles, bad plumbing, broken hinges on the pantry storage.

And most repairs coming out of my pocket.

A scraping chair caught my attention and Jack waved as he left the shop. I cleared his table as my assistants Johnnie and Olivia arrived for their shift; Lucy appeared a few minutes later when Jillian and the other ladies headed out.

The kitchen shifted into full work mode as my regular morning customers trickled in at a steady pace and I started a batch of maple fudge, pushing Johnson's strange behavior out of my head. Whatever was going on with my landlord would have to wait.

Chapter 2: Girls' Night, Bad Morning

"Bridget!" My best friend, Hannah Murphy, grinned at me from my doorstep, the faint twinkle of stars overhead. "All ready for girl's night?"

I smiled back. "Come in. I'm keeping the pizzas warm in the oven and just opened a bottle of wine. I also brought home a treat for us from the bakery."

She tromped into the hall and did a little twirl, pushing a stray lock of blonde hair behind her ear. I noticed she had dyed her usual side braid.

"I see you went with the pink streak, not purple."

"Yeah, I wanted something bolder and more outrageous." She smiled. "In fact, I almost went with neon green. You like it?" She shifted her head, swinging the bubble-gum pink braid.

"Love it. Glad you didn't go with the green. It's not your colour."

"I was hoping you'd like it. The pink spoke to me."

Then she went to the kitchen, leaving me to follow, grinning like the Cheshire cat. Hannah was the perfect friend and every day I was grateful for her honest, effervescent personality. We complimented each other seamlessly; two witches enjoying life.

In the kitchen, I set out plates for the pizza and took the wine glasses out of the cupboard, arranging everything beside the bakery box I brought home.

"Do I smell maple?" Hannah tried to peek inside the box, and I pushed her hand away.

"Be patient." She pouted and I took pity on her. "It's maple fudge."

"Ooooh, I love your fudge. And I could use a treat after the day I had. I swear all the difficult customers came into the bookstore today." She made a face. "I mean, how hard is it to understand that a bestselling book is sold out and you'll have to wait for the new order to come in?"

"Must be the day for difficult customers." I dished up the pizza and inhaled the divine smell.

"Do tell."

"Maybe later. I want to eat first. Let's take this delightful food into the living room and watch TV."

"OMG, this fudge is perfect. It melts in your mouth and the maple taste… Did you use your magic to make it taste so good?" Hannah's blissful face looked expectantly at me from the oversized armchair.

"What?" Snuggled on the sofa, I glared over my wine glass. "I have never used my magic to enhance my baking."

"Really?" Hannah gave me her *'don't lie to me'* look.

"Okay. Maybe I spelled the saucepans so I never burn the caramel, but that's good business. It's a nightmare to clean out burnt caramel, and sometimes it ruins the pan. I'm cutting costs there." I took a bite of my pepperoni pizza and ended the conversation.

"Have I offended your cooking sensibilities?" Hannah laughed before munching on her ham and pineapple slice; she adored that combination, and didn't care when people turned up their noses at her favourite topping.

A purr and a soft rub against my leg distracted me from a retort. Taffy, my short-haired orange tabby cat, waited at my feet, staring at me with innocent green eyes.

"Oh, he wants to be petted." Hannah reached out her hand. "Here Taffy, I'll scratch your ears." Taffy ignored her.

"Oh, please. He wants pepperoni." Staring down at the hopeful feline, I added, "But he knows he can't have pepperoni because it's bad for him. I'll give you a little melted cheese, you mooch." I pried off a sticky bit of cheese from the top, so it had no sauce, and held it out for my cat. He gobbled it before jumping on the opposite end of the sofa and curling up for a nap.

"See. All lovey-dovey until he gets his treat."

"So, a typical cat?"

I smiled. "Yeah, but I love him."

"He loves you, too. I mean, you did rescue him as a kitten."

"Best decision I ever made. After moving here, that is. I love having a pet. Never had one growing up."

"I still can't believe that." Hannah shook her head. "Your mother sounds like a piece of work."

"She called me last night." I tightened my jaw at the memory. "She still wants me to come home. Can you believe that? She won't accept the move is permanent. I'm not going back to Toronto."

Hannah snorted. "I don't get that. My mother is so supportive of everything I do, even when I came out, or when I moved in with Eva."

"Well, she was right about Eva. I'm glad you dumped her."

"Yes, good riddance to my ex, but don't change the subject. You need to stand up to your mother. I know you don't like to talk about your relationship, and avoid confronting her, but still…"

"It's not that easy." I sighed. "My mother is a control freak. Think Jillian, only on steroids. She sees my move as a sign of immaturity, rebellion against the coven. In a way, she's right, but I left to escape the expectations of being her daughter, of being the heir and legacy to the grand witch Vivian Redwood." I picked at the edge of my pizza slice. "Any confrontation is useless."

"Maybe it's time to cut ties? I don't know the woman, but the way you describe her, she sounds toxic. Family should be supportive, not make you miserable."

"Maybe, but it's complicated. She's convinced I'm a wayward daughter and need saving. To be fair, I tried my best for a while to live up to her view of me. She can't get past that.

I guess that's the thing with us. She'll never accept me living a life without her."

Not that I hadn't tried. For years I rebelled against my mother, especially as a teenager. Late nights, disobedience, and then a stint of practicing dark magic. I thought my mother's head would explode when she caught me with a forbidden text on the darker arts. She threatened to blacklist me, but packed me off to a strict magic academy instead. Worst two years of my life.

"Do you think she'll ever see you've changed? You've matured?"

Hannah's voice pulled me back from the unpleasant memories. "I'm always hoping, and constantly disappointed." I took a large sip of wine. "I should know better, but I don't."

"I'm sorry." Hannah reached out and patted my hand. "Mothers and daughters, right? It's never easy. But I wish she'd accept your decision and make things right."

My mother, give up control? Not likely.

I shrugged. "Probably won't happen. Few people defy the great Vivian Redwood. She'll keep trying to bring me back into the fold. You're right, one day I'll need to summon the courage to make a permanent break." I stared into the wine, swirling the alcohol, letting my anger and frustration twist.

"But not tonight." Hannah's gentle voice broke my morose thoughts.

"No. Tonight is for pizza and TV." I flicked on some gimmicky cooking show and we settled in to watch.

"So, we've missed you at the coven meetings." Hannah dropped her problematic comment in the middle of a crème brûlée disaster and I paused to see the drama play out before replying. Gave me time to form a diplomatic answer.

"Yeah, things with the shop have been hectic. Lots of problems and issues with the landlord."

"So, it's not because of Jillian Burke?"

Hannah never missed anything. "Well, maybe a bit. She wants me to be more active in the coven, pestered me to co-chair a committee with her, and work on a fundraiser." I sipped some wine to ease my irritation. "She was even in the bakery today, with Emily and Sarah. That was weird, actually."

"Why? Did Jillian say something?"

"Not to me, but Jeffery Johnson was there, and he and Jillian had words."

"Really? Interesting."

"You're not surprised? Why?"

"Just some gossip going around. He was doing some work for her or something, and it didn't measure up. I heard she fired him."

"That I believe. She's so fussy. Controlling, like my mother. That's probably why I've been avoiding her. She reminds me of all the stuck-up coven witches I left behind."

"I get that, and you shouldn't have to put up with her annoyance. Don't worry, I'll talk to Donna. She'll sort Jillian out."

"Um, I'm not sure that's a good idea." I loved her willingness to act as my buffer in the local coven, so I didn't have to deal with politics, but… I squirmed, feeling uncomfortable. "You've been great, helping me fit in with a new coven. I don't want you on Jillian's hit list, or to make enemies. I had enough of that in Toronto."

"Don't worry. Nobody in the coven likes Jillian much. We sort of tolerate her."

"Huh? I thought she was well-respected. A notable witch."

Hannah shook her head. "Not her, exactly, but her family. Her mother and grandmother, even her great-grandmother, were respected witches. Another coven, but still, she gets some legacy respect and a pass, I guess. That doesn't transfer into her being likeable, though."

"Oh, I get it. Sometimes it's who you know and family legacy." I understood those expectations and perceptions all too well.

"Yeah, covens around here have deep roots. A lot of heritage and extended, interconnected lineages. The Easthaven Bay coven has been here a long time. You should peruse the records sometime. You might be surprised at our connections." Hannah smirked. "And speaking of connections, have you seen Jack lately?"

"Oh, look, the judging has started." I brusquely changed the subject and peered intently at the TV.

Hannah suspected my reluctant attraction to Jack, and I wasn't in the mood for her curiosity. But she wouldn't let it go.

"I know he stopped by your shop this morning. Did he ask about anything?"

"No." I shot her a look. What would Jack MacNeil want to ask me? "He ordered coffee and a doughnut, then got into it with my landlord."

"What?" Hannah looked surprised. "He argued with Mr. Johnson? That's not—how did that happen? Was it part of what occurred with Jillian?"

"No, this was before. Johnson barged into the shop and we had words. Jack decided I needed defending or something and jumped into the middle of it, but Johnson lit into him. Then Johnson took his sour mood out on the ladies and I kicked him out. Jack left shortly after."

"Oh." Hannah seemed disappointed. "Nothing else?"

I frowned, remembering. "He did mention the community supper... Wait, was something supposed to happen?" I eyed her suspiciously. Ever since her breakup last year, Hannah had been on a matchmaking kick.

She smiled. "Maybe, but I guess we will never know."

"What are you up to now?" I was annoyed. "Just because your love life went sideways, don't fiddle with mine."

"Come on! My love life didn't go sideways, I left a bad relationship. End of story. Yeah, I'm a little gun shy, so forgive me for wanting to live vicariously through you. Besides, it's not as if you have a love life, despite my attempts to set you up. Jack might provide that. You two have been circling each other for ages."

"I don't think so. Yeah, we're friendly, sort of, but just because the guy likes old sci-fi movies, doesn't mean he's dating material. He's too conventional for his own good. I don't need a guy that likes to play white knight with women. No matter how good-looking he is."

Hannah laughed. "Methinks you protest too much. I know you're attracted to him. Every time we go to his bar, it's when he's working shifts as the bartender. I've seen you staring at him when he isn't looking."

"I do not stare!"

"Yes, you do, and why not? He's a catch, being part owner of the bar. Not to mention gorgeous. You should go for it. Even if it's only for some fun. You could use a little excitement and fun."

"Oh, please. My life is fine. Besides, with our schedules, when would we even get together?"

"Ah-ha! I knew it. You have thought about getting together with him."

I blushed, rolling my eyes. Hannah looked smug, but let the matter drop. We watched the end of the show and the poor crème brûlée baker got kicked out of the competition.

A late night caused me to miss my alarm and wake up a half-hour later than usual the next morning. I regretted drinking that last glass of wine as I scrambled to get ready, and a throbbing headache mixed with a sour stomach had me reaching for my special witch's brew hangover cure before eating a quick breakfast. After downing two cups of coffee to stay awake, I made sure Taffy was fed before rushing out to open the bakery. At least I wouldn't have to worry about traffic this early, and made good time on the drive over.

I noticed the faint smell of maple when I entered the shop.

Odd. Was there a spill I missed? I hope something didn't get left out.

As I tucked my purse under the counter and scanned the empty display cases, another thought occurred to me.

Oh no. I hope the fridge or freezer didn't die on me.

I raced into the kitchen only to pull up short. My guts churned in nauseous shock; that coffee I drank seemed like a bad idea now. I choked back the rising bile, along with the urge to shriek, and stared, my mind racing. Jeffery Johnson lay on my floor by the industrial fridge, unmoving and glassy eyed, surrounded by scattered chunks of maple fudge. There was even a half-eaten piece by his mouth.

I stood there like an idiot, gaping, willing this to be a dream, or a joke, until my senses finally kicked in. I crept over and knelt down by the body. His face was reddish, but he wasn't breathing, and discoloured patches of fluid were dried around his bluish lips. I checked a cold rubbery wrist for a pulse. Nothing. He was dead. I scrambled away, gagging.

What do I do? What do I do?

Taking deep breaths, I slowly backed out of the kitchen, before racing to grab my purse and my phone. I called 911 as I dashed out of the bakery.

After the cops from the nearest RCMP station arrived and cordoned off the place, I called my assistants to tell them not to show up for work. The police took my initial statement, asking me when I arrived, what did I touch, did I know the victim? I babbled most of my answers. The whole situation was surreal, like I was in a crime show.

Except it's real.

It didn't take long for the looky-loos to start milling and I was glad the cops kept them at a distance; the attention and sympathetic looks of my neighbours had me squirming with self-conscious embarrassment. I spotted Jack in the crowd, shoulders hunched, hands shoved in his pockets; part of me wanted him to come over, but he turned and hurried off when he noticed me watching. I tried not to feel disappointed or abandoned.

Like he would rush over and comfort me.

Overwhelmed, I stared at the bakery, trying to ignore the onlookers, but still heard the chatter, *felt* them watching the crime unit and the police officers do their jobs. Teeth clenched, a headache throbbed at my temples despite the hangover cure. I endured the tense buzz of gossip until a medical examiner wheeled out the body; then you could hear a pin drop in the silence.

A stern-faced officer approached me. "I'm Constable Cooper, we'll be closing down the bakery until further notice. If possible, we'd like you to come with us for a more detailed interview."

A little uneasy, I replied, "Sure. Whatever you need." I swallowed, my mouth and throat dry, wondering what was going on. "Poor Mr. Johnson. Did he have a heart attack or something?"

"The cause of death is currently undetermined." The officer did not elaborate, only opened a squad car and ushered me into the back seat.

I sat straight-backed, hugging the purse on my lap, suddenly feeling like a criminal, as we drove to the RCMP station. Out the window, Easthaven Bay's scenery flashed by, the quaint seaside town views somehow making everything worse. This wasn't how my day was supposed to go. Even dead, my landlord was causing me trouble.

How did Johnson end up dead in my bakery? Why was he even there?

Can this get any worse?

Chapter 3: A Maple Spirit

Sitting across from a RCMP sergeant, my headache still beating a rhythm inside my head, I nursed a kindly provided coffee and resisted the urge to fidget in my chair. Fidgeting made you seem guilty of something, right?

The officer cleared his throat slightly. "I'm Sergeant Boudreau and before we start, I'd like to inform you this interview is being recorded. You are here as a witness, so we can get a better idea of events. No need to be nervous."

I relaxed, trying not to yawn, some of the tension easing out of my shoulders. I loosened my grip on the edge of the table and focused on the interview. "Um, okay. What would you like to know?"

"First, do you have any idea why Mr. Johnson would have been in the bakery either late last evening or early this morning?"

I shook my head, instantly regretting it. "It was a shock. I mean, he's the landlord, so he has the keys, but he's never entered without letting me know or my being there." I frowned. "At least I don't think he has."

"Do you have reason to believe he's entered without letting you know before today?"

"Um, no," I sipped my coffee and gathered my thoughts. I really wanted a nap. "He has been acting odd lately, though. Dodging my calls and texts, not making repairs or putting them off. Something was going on with him. Don't know why that would lead him to enter the bakery without telling anyone."

"I see. He was causing trouble for you, then?"

"Not trouble, exactly. More like shirking his duties. I was thinking of seeing a lawyer about my rights."

"Had you been arguing?"

I nodded, tension creeping back into my neck, and a sour sensation forming in my stomach. "Yes, a little. Yesterday morning we had a disagreement."

The officer scribbled in his notebook. "And what time was that?"

"Not long after I opened the bakery to customers, probably around 8:15 or 8:20 AM. He had ignored my calls about a repair, then suddenly showed up to talk. He was in a bad mood."

"Did he seem worried? Anxious?"

I shook my head. "More argumentative. He yelled at me and picked fights with two of my customers."

"Interesting. Which customers?"

"Um, well," I hesitated, disliking the feeling of getting someone into possible trouble.

"Names, Miss Redwood. Please."

I sighed. "Jack MacNeil and Jillian Burke. He was also rude to Sarah Clarke and Emily Acker."

"Thank you. We'll check that out." He scribbled something down in his notes.

I restrained myself from wriggling and ventured questions of my own. "Do you know how he died? Was it a heart attack?"

The officer looked up. "Nothing conclusive yet. Preliminary investigations are suggestive, and ongoing." He stared at me.

I licked my lips, my mouth feeling dry. "Um, suggestive? What does that mean?"

"The medical examiner still has to determine the cause of death."

"Oh. Chances are he died from some health thing, right? I mean he smoked and took terrible care of himself."

"It is too soon to comment on that, but that is a possibility. There are a few anomalies that need to be cleared up. For instance, the fudge found surrounding the body. Can you shed some light on that, Miss Redwood?"

"What? No. I placed the leftover fudge in the fridge before I locked up. Maybe he was after a midnight snack?" I rubbed the back of my neck. "Why are you interested in the fudge?"

Then the officer dropped a bombshell of a question.

"Is there any way the fudge could have been contaminated with toxic substances?"

What is he saying? Toxic substances?

"No. It was perfectly fine. What are you implying?"

"I'm not implying anything. We are looking into all possibilities."

What possibilities? Are they thinking...

"Do you know if Mr. Johnson had any enemies? Someone who would do him harm?"

Fighting a sudden panic, I babbled, "Lots of people. Half the town, probably. No one liked him much."

What did all this mean? I shook my head, trying to comprehend the possibility of someone harming Johnson. Could anyone in our town hate him that much?

"I see. Does anyone specific come to mind?"

"No. He was an unpleasant man."

"I see." More scribbling in his notebook. "Now, can I get a clearer idea of last night's timeline? Where were you? Did you go out, stay home?"

Were they looking for an alibi? Did I need an alibi? Am I a suspect?

"Um," I swallowed, feeling like a mouse facing a cat. "I locked up the bakery around 8 PM. We close at six, but there's cleanup and prep for the next day. My assistants were with me, so you can check with them."

He nodded and wrote in his notes again.

"Then I stopped at the liquor store and bought a bottle of wine—"

"Any particular reason for that, Miss Redwood?" He smiled as he interrupted, yet I still felt I was being judged on my every word.

"Girl's night. After I bought the wine, I was at Joe's Pizzeria and picked up my order of two pizzas—"

"And what time was that?"

I suppressed a scowl. *This would go a lot faster if you'd stop interrupting.*

"About 8:30 or so. I was out of there and back home before 9 PM."

More scribbling. "Then what?"

"My friend Hannah Murphy arrived. We ate pizza, drank wine and watched TV until about midnight, maybe closer to 1 AM." I took a breath and hurried on before he interrupted again. "Then she walked home and I went to bed. I woke up around 5 AM, a little later than normal, but I arrived at the bakery before six."

"Very good, Miss Redwood. That's sufficient for now. We'll double-check everything of course, but you are free to go. However, we may be in touch with further questions."

I stood and grabbed my purse, headed to the door, turning around at the last minute. "Do you know when the bakery will be cleared? When can I open again?"

"It could be a few days; we'll let you know." He nodded at the door, and I knew I was dismissed. I hurried out of the station, calling Hannah to come pick me up. Sliding the phone back in my purse, I leaned against the building, my eyes closed, trying to make sense of everything. Then a familiar voice jerked me back to reality.

"Bridget. Are you okay?"

I opened my eyes to see Jack standing in front of me, a look of concern etched in his expression. A complete shift from his earlier behaviour. I guess he was back in his white knight mode.

Why is he here?

Jack shifted his feet, sliding his hands in his pockets. "What did the police say? Why did they want to question you? Is something going on?"

I scowled, crossing my arms; the last thing I needed was another interrogation. I resorted to sarcasm to combat my inner chaos. "Mr. Johnson died in my shop. I think something is going on."

Jack took a step back, clearly surprised by my annoyance. "Hey, sorry. I was worried is all. I mean, the police took you away. I was afraid you were in trouble."

Regretting my rudeness, I blurted, "They were asking me questions, wanted to know where I was and if Johnson had enemies. I think they are investigating the death as suspicious." I reached out a hand. "I don't know what's going on."

Jack frowned, and stepped away, muttering, "I have to go." He turned and hurried into the police station, leaving me staring at his retreating back. I lowered my hand and swallowed the rejection.

What is with that guy?

I slumped, staring back at the road, waiting for Hannah to pull up in her car.

I was more than ready to go home.

"I know your maple fudge is to die for, but Jeffery Johnson took it to extremes."

Hannah and I were sprawled on the couch drinking last night's wine and eating leftover pizza for lunch. The cat was asleep in his basket.

"Don't mention my fudge. It wasn't the fudge. I think the police suspect it wasn't natural or an accident, but that can't be what happened. Everyone ate that fudge and no one got sick. Nothing was in the fudge. Whatever killed him, it wasn't the fudge. Unless he choked on it or something."

Maybe if I keep saying it, it will be true.

"Hey, of course it wasn't. I was making a joke." Hannah patted my hand, her face contrite. "A bad one, I'm sorry. What exactly did the police say?"

"They were vague about everything. They mentioned toxic substances, so maybe they think food poisoning? Or… It's all so weird. What was he doing there after hours?" I sighed. "I'm getting a strange feeling about this whole thing."

"Strange feeling how? Witch-type feelings or regular suspicions?"

"Regular." Even as I said it, I wasn't sure. Maybe something *was* prickling at my witch radar. "At least, I think so."

"Hope they're wrong about it not being an accident or him keeling over from a heart attack." Hannah nibbled on her pizza slice. "Although a mystery might liven things up in this town. Everyone is already buzzing about what happened, how Johnson died. I've heard theories from suicide to murder and everything in-between."

"I'm surprised the town doesn't consider me the number one suspect in how he died."

"What? Why? Everybody I know likes you."

"He ate my fudge, then died. It can't have been the fudge, but yet… Plus, I'm still considered an outsider. That girl from away."

Hannah laughed. "Being from away doesn't automatically make you a suspect in someone's death. Half the town thinks he deserved it anyway. That some cosmic karma got him."

"Maybe it did." I shrugged. "I've seen odder things happen."

"At least you won't have to deal with him as a landlord anymore. I wonder who will inherit his properties? He wasn't married and had no kids as far as I know."

A chill ran down my spine. I hadn't thought of that. "Hannah, what if I lose the space? Have to move the bakery? There's no guarantee any new landlord will uphold the lease. I could get evicted. Or get slapped with a rent hike. That's the perfect location. I don't want to move!" That last bit came as a wail, channeling all my pent-up emotion.

"Hey, now. Don't get ahead of yourself. We don't know what will happen. Besides, it'll be weeks, maybe months before any probate is settled. If the worst happens, there will be time to deal with it, make contingency plans."

I took a couple of deep breaths, and calmed myself down, blocking the thought of my mother's inevitable *'I told you so'* if things failed. If I had to change locations, so be it. There were other places to rent here. My customers would follow. I hoped they would, at least.

Why did Jeffery Johnson have to die?

Then, as if on cue, the air shimmered with light, a blue radiance coalescing in front of the far wall, and the entire room vibrated in mystical energy. Both Hannah and I sat up, senses alert with alarm, as we watched the incorporeal, dishevelled ghost of Jeffery Johnson form in my living room while the smell of almonds and maple filled the room. Taffy woke up immediately and hissed at the apparition. My cat jumped from his basket, stalked around the ghost, glaring and meowing his displeasure. I stared in disbelief.

Now I'm being haunted by the guy?

I glanced at Hannah; she didn't say a word. As we watched, Johnson phased in and out as if he couldn't anchor in one plane or the other. Not uncommon for new apparitions, but nausea-inducing to watch, like those spinning hypnotic swirls.

Reaching out a hand, Johnson spat a few garbled, unintelligible words until the apparition stabilized for a few seconds, and the shimmering essence of my landlord wheezed, "*Spells, witch, danger...*", before fading in and out again. I heard the word "*murder,*" and then as clear as day I could see him. He shouted, "*Jack is...*"

Then he disappeared.

Hannah looked at me, stunned.

"What the heck was that about?"

Chapter 4: Sifting Through Clues

With the bakery closed, I slept in the next morning, at least until 8 AM when someone started pounding on my door. I threw on a robe, thumped down the stairs and answered the insistent knocking.

Hannah smiled at me. She sported a large tote bag.

"Don't look like such a grump. I brought breakfast." She pulled a plastic container out of her bag. "I stopped by Mom's this morning and she insisted I bring you homemade egg and bacon sandwiches on toasted bagels. With her special sauce." Hannah brushed past me as my mouth watered. "And I don't have work today, so you're stuck with me."

Closing the door, I said, "I'll make the coffee."

The smell of bacon and coffee soon mingled as we enjoyed our breakfast and ignored any mention of what happened. I knew that was why Hannah stopped by; she wanted to talk about it last night, but I shut her down. I needed time to think, and bless her, she gave it to me. Now the reprieve was over.

After wiping the bacon grease from my mouth and slurping the last of my coffee, I said, "Let's hear it. I know you're dying to give me your thoughts on our ghost appearance."

Hannah laughed. "Come on, what did you expect? I love drama, and this is big. A ghost shows up here and drops the bombshell he was murdered. And mumbles about spells and witches and danger. And that bit about Jack? Is he involved in this? Is he in danger? Are we? Do you think Jack is a secret witch? How did Johnson even know about witches? Or spells. This could be major."

"Major trouble, maybe. Which I don't want." I took a few breaths, trying to sort Hannah's whirlwind of questions. "We have no way of knowing what Johnson was spouting last night was true or what it meant. We only heard bits and pieces. For all we know he could have been trying to say he *wasn't* murdered."

"Oh, please." Hannah scoffed at me. "You know it takes serious trauma to keep the dead tied to this plane. Ghosts don't appear unless there is unfinished business. Like being murdered."

"Or sudden unexpected accidents. Like choking on fudge or having a heart attack while sneaking around where you shouldn't be. Johnson was up to something, sure, but that doesn't mean murder." I knew I was reaching, because all my instincts were screaming to stay out of it.

"That doesn't explain the mention of spells or witches. Johnson wasn't part of our world."

"Maybe he watched an old movie before he died." I ducked my head as I said it.

Hannah gave me her *'are you serious'* look. "Wow, that was lame." She added, "So, how do you explain away Jack?"

"Um… Okay, I can't. A ghost came and dumped some mumbo-jumbo on me—on us. That doesn't mean we should get involved. I know how these things go. Reports and scrutiny, coven politics and a whole lot of headaches and trouble. If he was murdered, and I'm not saying he was, let the police handle it. The ghost will be satisfied once they arrest a killer. If there is a killer."

"And in the meantime? The ghost came here for a reason. He's not going to go away. You'll have to handle it eventually, so it could be best to face it now. Maybe you should do a summoning?"

"No!" That was the last thing I wanted. I wanted to ignore it, yet I knew Hannah was right. For whatever reason, Johnson's ghost latched on to me. He'd return. I sighed.

"No summoning, but if he comes back, we'll try to figure out what he wants. Don't get the coven Council involved. Not yet anyway. I'd rather find out what's going on first."

"Deal." Hannah smirked and poured both of us another cup of coffee. "So, where do we start? The obvious place would be the bakery, but that's off-limits. Still, Johnson was there for some reason before he died. Can you think of any motive for why he'd be sneaking around in the middle of the night? I mean, he's not the cat burglar type."

"Yeah. I've been thinking about that." I sighed before continuing. "Wondering if maybe it's connected to stuff at the shop needing repairs lately."

Hannah frowned. "Do you think Johnson was sabotaging you?"

"Maybe." I shrugged.

"Why?"

"That's a harder question. To break the lease? Get me to move out?"

"Is there anything special about the building? A reason Johnson would be skulking around, undermining things? It's old, I know that."

"It dates back to the early 1900s, I think, but nothing noteworthy unless you count the rumours of it being a rumrunner hideout in the 1920s."

"Yeah, half the buildings in town have those stories attached." Hannah grinned. "Half the families too." Then she sighed. "So, no clues there, I guess. I brought some books on coven history and some records on witch lineage. We can check to see if Johnson's family was ever listed or involved in the coven. Could be that's what the ghost was trying to say."

"Worth a shot, I guess. Not much else we can do until the ghost shows up again." What was I saying? With any luck, I'd never see that ghost again. At least this would keep Hannah occupied.

Hannah got to work while I showered and dressed, and then I joined her. We poured over the books all morning but found nothing to indicate Johnson or his family had any connections to the witches of Easthaven Bay.

Hannah slammed the last book shut with a sigh. "Dead ends. No pun intended."

"That's because we're fumbling around in the dark. We don't know what he meant. Or even how he died. Did he choke? Or have a heart attack? Or maybe he had an allergic reaction." I paused, not really wanting to voice it out loud. Yet, it needed to be said. "Or was poisoned." I sighed. "I hope I'm wrong about that."

"It is a possibility, but nothing's for certain." She patted my hand. "I think I jumped the gun. Let's give it a rest and go out. Do a little shopping. I know you've been wanting to check out the new crystals at Silver Trinkets and Gifts, and I need some candles. Then we can have lunch at that new café. Besides, I don't think we can do more unless there's another ghost sighting."

"Sounds like a plan." I wasn't sure I wanted to go out, but at least Hannah dropped the whole investigation kick. For now. And maybe a distraction with lunch and shopping would be good. So we packed away the books and the empty food containers and headed out.

Hannah and I parted ways after lunch and I walked home, thoughts of ghosts and murder blissfully banished under a small assortment of purchases that included three amethyst crystals, some spices, and a new novelty whisk. Until

I arrived at my front door and found Jack MacNeil standing on my doorstep.

"Hey. That's luck. I was about to leave. No one answered my knock."

"Yeah. I went out to lunch with Hannah." I stood there like an idiot, my heart beating like a bongo drum, house keys dangling from my hand.

Why is he here?

"That's nice. Good you have someone, after everything that happened yesterday." Jack smiled, a sheepish grin.

Oh my, he still looked hot even when he was embarrassed.

"That's kind of why I'm here. I'm worried about you. I need to talk about Johnson."

Annoyance and elation hit me in equal measure; I couldn't get away from Johnson, but Jack was concerned about me. Again. For a moment I wasn't sure what to do; I didn't want to discuss Johnson or the murder, yet…

Should I make excuses or invite him in?

Moving past him I unlocked the door.

"Come in."

Jack followed me inside.

Chapter 5: New Ingredients

I dropped my purse and shucked off my coat. "Let's talk in the kitchen. I'll make coffee."

I led the way and Jack settled onto a stool by the counter as I took mugs from the cupboard. I busied myself with preparations to quell my nerves; my stomach fluttered so much it felt as if an army of butterflies were fighting a war. A silence settled between us, drifting into a strange, palpable tension, and as I carried the mugs to the counter, I prayed not to drop them from my trembling fingers.

Why does he have this effect on me?

Neither of us said anything as we sipped our coffee, staring at each other across the kitchen counter. Taffy rubbed up against Jack's leg, angling for pets or an ear rub. Which was odd, because he only acted that way towards witches, and was almost never friendly to visitors.

I scowled at my cat, somehow feeling he was traitorous, and took a breath. Someone needed to start the conversation. I asked, "Why do you want to talk about Johnson?"

Jack bent down and scratched Taffy's ears for a few minutes before he answered. "Like I said, I'm worried about you. You're a nice girl, Bridget. You shouldn't get dragged into this mess, whatever it is." He took a sip of coffee, and then another.

Inwardly, I smiled, watching him drink. *He thinks I'm nice.*

Jack looked at me with his sheepish little smile. "I hope we're good enough friends that I can offer you advice. Stay as far away as you can from whatever happens with the investigation. Things are… Well, there was more to Johnson than most people know and I wouldn't want you pulled into his schemes."

I think it's too late for that. Stupid ghost.

I frowned as a thought occurred to me, and I tapped my fingernail against my cup. "It's nice you're looking out for me, but how do you know what Johnson was into? Why were you arguing in my shop the morning before he died? Were you two involved in some shady business?"

Jack shrugged. "Johnson's business was mostly legitimate, you know, despite his bad reputation. I don't want you being associated with that, though."

His evasive answer didn't sit well with me and his protective attitude turned sour. Why was he really here? "What's going on, Jack? Do you know why Johnson snuck into my shop that night?"

He shook his head. "Whatever it was, it couldn't have been good. Or legal. If you poke around it might lead to trouble or you getting hurt. Maybe it's best if you stay out of it."

Now I was more suspicious. "Why would I get hurt? The guy died in my shop, but it's nothing to do with me."

"Good. You should keep it that way. Murder isn't something to be played with."

That set off alarm bells. "Who said it was murder?"

Jack chuckled. "The town rumour mill, that's who. If it's true, Johnson was into some dangerous stuff. Dangerous, even for someone like you."

Wait. What?

"Someone like me? What does that mean?"

"I think we both know the answer. The company you keep gives you away." Jack smirked and slid off his stool, headed for the front door. I chased him, but he waved me away, saying, "Think about what I said, Bridget." The door slammed shut on his words.

What was that all about? And what did he mean 'for someone like me'? He couldn't know…

I raced back and grabbed my phone from my purse, dialling Hannah.

"Get your butt over here, now! We have to talk."

Hannah made record time in arriving, entering my house, breathless. "What's the emergency?"

"Does Jack know about witches? Specifically, that I'm a witch?"

"Hey, what? The MacNeils aren't part of the coven. Or associated with it, as far as I know. I've never seen them mentioned in the histories. What the heck brought this on?"

"Jack paid me a visit. Warned me that involving myself in Johnson's death could be dangerous. Even for 'someone like me'."

"Jack warned you off? That's suspicious. Yet it's a bit of a reach to think he knows you are a witch."

"Then why phrase it that way? Like me, how? A woman, a baker? Neither of them would make Jack think I could deal with a dangerous situation."

Hannah frowned. "You have a point. The phrasing is odd."

I took a breath, glad Hannah was finally getting it. "It was the way he said it, too. Like he knew a secret. There's more to Jack than we assumed. Is there anyone we can quietly talk to that might know if he's involved in the witch community?"

"I thought you didn't want to get involved."

"I don't, but it might be too late. I'd rather know what I'm dealing with than be blindsided."

"Fair enough. Shirley might know. She'll keep her mouth shut if we ask. She also has a sweet tooth."

"I have some brownies in the freezer. Will that make an acceptable bribe?"

"Perfect."

We arrived at Shirley's house with a container of thawing brownies, questions, and uncertain expectations. After a quick knock, we were ushered inside with a demonstrative greeting and a delightful thank you for the brownies. We plonked ourselves down on the flowery-patterned couch while Shirley settled in the matching armchair.

"So," Shirley eyed us with an amused grin, "what can I do for you girls?"

"Um…" I hesitated, unsure how to begin. "Well—"

"What's the dirt on Jeffery Johnson and Jack MacNeil?" Hannah spat it out and continued on, "Did Johnson know about the existence of witches? Does Jack? Are the MacNeils some part of the community? We've never heard of any connection, but evidence points to them being involved. We need to know."

"Do you now?" Shirley chuckled. "You young people. Always wanting to know things. Well, let me tell you, rooting around buried secrets might get you into trouble. Tell me your reasons for asking these questions and then we'll see about answers."

It was my turn to be direct. "We think Johnson was killed and Jack's involved somehow." I took a breath, deciding to trust Shirley. "Johnson's ghost appeared to us, mumbling about spells and witches and murder. I would appreciate you not saying anything about this. For now, at least."

"Ooooh, now. Ghosts put a different slant on things. Wouldn't surprise me though if he got himself killed. Johnson was always up to no good. Runs in that family." Shirley leaned down and plucked some knitting out of a bag beside her chair, and the clack of her needles echoed under her next words. "You're right, though, best to keep this quiet for now. Some in the coven might not appreciate you taking an interest." She nodded, clicking her needles as we waited patiently.

"None of Johnson's family are witches, but they know we exist; they tend to be leeches, the lot of them. Jeffery Johnson was the same, hiring himself out as an errand boy to some of the coven witches. Getting them this and that under the table. Circumventing the rules and the politics, you know."

"Do you know any names of the ones he worked for?" I ventured. "It would be useful to know who to look out for, if there's more trouble."

"I might, I might." Shirley nodded. "Could be I'll make a list and send it over your way later."

I wanted to press but knew it would be pointless. She would do it or she wouldn't.

"Don't know anything about Johnson getting killed, poor soul." Shirley paused, giving a moment of silence for the dead. "The trouble between the Johnsons and the MacNeils, now that goes way back. Neither family were a respected bunch back then. Of course, the MacNeils rose up in the community quicker than the Johnsons and are better esteemed now. That probably helped fuel the feud."

"Feud?"

"Yeah, there's been bad blood between them since…let's see, my Gran said they were involved in the rum-running, so it must have been the 20s. Yes, that's when it happened. That's when Angus MacNeil destroyed George Johnson's boat.

Rigged it to explode. That's how Angus and his family got kicked out of the coven."

"What?" Hannah nearly shrieked. "The MacNeils are witches?"

"Were witches. At least officially. That boat incident got them banned from the coven and their names taken out of the records. No MacNeil has been formally recognized as a witch since, but plenty of them still practice. Including Jack. Got their ears in the coven too. I know a few members who let the MacNeils know what's what in witch business."

"I can't believe it." Hannah looked stunned, sucking in a breath. "We have rogue witches in Easthaven Bay?"

Shirley chuckled. "Official, rogue, it's all for show. Keeps the witches in line, especially the younger ones. If rogues stay away from the darker magicks and don't draw unwanted attention, our coven mostly turns a blind eye."

Hannah slumped in her chair. "I don't believe it."

It didn't surprise me. I'd seen worse in coven politics. A few quiet rogues outside a coven was a fairly common thing.

Then Shirley dropped another bombshell. "Bet Johnson was pestering Jack for that map."

I stared. "Map? What map?"

Hannah glanced up, her disillusionment banished. "A treasure map?"

Shirley shrugged. "Maybe. No one but the MacNeils really know. I heard Johnson was sniffing around about old maps a few months back. A good chance if there were problems between him and Jack, they revolved around that."

"Oh, this got more interesting." Her initial shock forgotten, Hannah brightened. "Secrets, murder, now mysterious maps."

I was glad someone was enjoying this. "So, how did this map end up with the MacNeils? Why would Johnson be interested?"

"Well now," Shirley put down her knitting and looked me in the eye, "long been a rumour something more than rum-running was going on during the days of Angus MacNeil. That old Angus and George Johnson made a pact, smuggled in some magical artifact. That Angus stole it and made a cryptic map that revealed the spot where he hid it." Shirley grinned. "My Gran used to tell me some tales. 'Bout how they found a phoenix feather or a Djinn's lamp. One time it was a map to a pirate treasure. Once, it was the map to the true location of the Oak Island treasure." Shirley chuckled. "Gran never could keep her stories straight. She was one for a good yarn-spinning, she was."

I closed my eyes. This whole situation began to sound like a bad, made-for-TV adventure movie. We had a lot of rumours and possibilities, but were no closer to knowing why a man died in my bakery or why his ghost manifested at my house. We weren't getting anywhere, so I stood.

"Thanks, Shirley. I appreciate your time and the information."

"No worries, luv. Just be careful. You might be stepping in a hornet's nest."

I nodded and gestured to Hannah that we were leaving. Once outside, she bubbled over.

"Can you believe it! The MacNeils are really witches."

"Shush! Do you want someone to hear you?"

"Oh, right. Last thing we want is another rumour mill."

"Yeah, let's wait until we get back to my house." I wanted time to think anyway.

We lapsed into silence until we arrived.

As I unlocked the front door, I turned back to Hannah. "We should make a plan—" Then I stopped, seeing the stunned look on her face. I slowly turned around.

The ghost of Jeffery Johnson hovered in my hallway.

Chapter 6: Secret Pieces

"Get in, quick," I hissed. Hannah and I rushed inside, shutting the door. The ghost immediately started shaking and moaned softly. Taffy hissed at him, his fur bristling, his paws scuffing at the floor.

"*Murdered me, murdered me...why did ...she won't stop...beware!*" The last word was shouted and our apparition disappeared in a flash of light.

"Jeez, lay on the melodrama." Hannah huffed, exhaling loudly.

I picked up Taffy, soothing his ruffled feelings. "Ghosts aren't known for long conversations. It's usually confused snippets and warnings." I headed to the kitchen as Hannah scurried after me.

"Wait. Have you done this before? Had ghost sightings?"

"Not personal ones like this." I put a wriggling Taffy down after giving him a treat. "Back in Toronto, I was part of investigation teams for other hauntings. You'd be surprised how many novice witches accidentally conjure up ghosts."

"Not around here they don't, but I guess you know how to banish a ghost then. You could make this all go away?"

Hannah said that slowly, tilting her head and giving me a funny look.

I shook my head. "Not that easy. You know that. Banishing an unwilling ghost is dangerous."

The tension in Hannah's face eased. "Good. At least you won't do something stupid."

No. As much as I wanted to make this mess disappear, being reckless and irresponsible wouldn't help. "I'll be good. I'd never hear the end of it from my mother if I wasn't." I grinned and started brewing some tea. "At least we have another clue."

"We do?" Hannah sounded confused.

"Yeah. Didn't you hear Johnson? He said, 'she.' That means there's a woman involved. And I'll bet that *she* is on that list of witches Shirley mentioned."

"Hmm. Possible." Hannah rummaged in her purse and pulled out a pen and notebook. "Let's make a list of what we know."

She started scribbling. "One, Johnson was probably murdered. How, we don't know. Two, Jack was involved with Johnson, possibly over an old treasure map. Three, Johnson's murderer may have been a woman, possibly a witch." She looked up. "That sound right?"

"You forgot there's a spell or spells involved somehow."

"Oh, yeah." She hastily wrote something down. "There, 'spell involved' is on the list."

"None of it adds up to anything. If Johnson's stupid ghost keeps showing up, the least he could do is be helpful. The man is as maddening in death as he was in life."

"Well, yeah. It's not much, but it's something. Let's start with the map. Does it factor in at all? Or is it a tall tale?"

"Could be a tale. Leave it on the list, though. Mr. Johnson was interested in maps and Shirley did mention his family were part of the original scheme, whatever it was."

"Why go after it now? Presumably, the map story was known to the Johnson family for a while, so why was Jeffery Johnson after the MacNeil map all of a sudden? To the point where it may have gotten him killed?"

I frowned. Hannah had a point. "The mystery woman maybe? Johnson did like money. Maybe she wanted to buy the map and offered to pay Johnson if he could get it."

"I suppose." Hannah didn't look convinced. "That doesn't seem like a great motive for murder though. And how are you involved? Or at least your shop."

"You're right, that— Hey, wait a minute. The shop. We can check the blueprints for the place. I still have them around here somewhere from the renovations." That had been the deal when I rented. I could retool the space to fit my needs.

"Well, what are we waiting for? Let's go hunt up those designs."

Hannah jumped up and grabbed my arm. The next thing I knew, we were ransacking drawers, cupboards and closets to find the plans. They ended up being tucked away on top of some books in my office bookshelf. We spread them across the floor and hunkered down to study them.

Hannah glanced over at me. "What are we looking for?"

"The reason Johnson was in my shop the night he died. He must have been searching for something, right? So, maybe there is a hidden room, something that was bricked over, or generally out-of-place. We both know the bakery. We need to look for any major differences between the building and the blueprints."

"Wouldn't any weird anomaly have been discovered in the remodel?"

"It wasn't an extensive redesign and the basic structure is the same. We didn't knock any walls down or anything."

We studied the plans, but nothing leapt out at us. "I don't see anything strange."

"Well, shoot." Hannah sat back, leaning against a chair. "Stupid plans." She glared at the blueprints and nudged them with her shoe. A corner rolled up and Hannah inhaled sharply. "Wait. These aren't the original plans. Look at the date on the back. It says 1977."

"So?"

"So, maybe the original plans are different. You couldn't have been the first person to renovate this place. We need to view the originals."

"Where are we going to find older copies of these blueprints?"

Hannah laughed. "The library, of course! My home away from home."

A quick excursion found us at the town library, a cozy two-storey building near the wharf district. The librarian on duty chatted with Hannah about books, before helping us find what we wanted and escorting us to a private room in the back. A cool salty spring breeze drifted in the open window.

"Let me know if you need anything else." The librarian nodded and left us alone to study a copy of my bakery's blueprints from 1919.

We rolled out both sets of blueprints and laid them out, side by side for comparison.

"Good thing the local Heritage Society had these stored here."

"They have an extensive collection, here and at the town hall," Hannah replied. "That would have been our next stop if we struck out here. I don't think it matters. I'm not seeing much of a difference. I guess there isn't a…"

"That's odd."

"What?" Hannah leaned in.

"This back alcove, near the rear door." I stabbed my finger on the 1919 blueprint. "Right there, it looks like an alcove juts out from the back entrance. It's not showing in the 70s plan and there's no alcove in the bakery. I don't remember the workers sealing it up." I sat up straight in my chair, a realization dawning. "In fact, I don't remember it at all. No recessed area, only a wall."

"That doesn't make sense? You must walk by the area every day."

"I do, yet until I saw it drawn on the plans, I would have sworn there was nothing there but a straight wall. Look at the more recent copy of the blueprints. There is a wall shown; the recess is outside, but that's wrong. How is that possible? You can't make part of a building disappear, unless—"

Hannah and I stared at each other and exclaimed, "A concealment spell."

We both lapsed into silence for a moment, before Hannah whispered, "That's crazy."

I nodded, my brain trying to make sense of what we learned.

How did I not notice?

I inhaled and let my breath out slowly. "I never had a whiff of magic. It would take a powerful spell to be that invisible. And long-lasting too, if we think it's related to the whole MacNeil and Johnson feud."

"Do you think that was what Johnson was searching for?"

"Maybe. Probably." I closed my eyes, thinking. "Does the library have any historic records for the bakery? Like who owned it back in the 20s?"

"They might, although we should check the Historical Society's website first. Melissa, who works in the Town Hall records office, set it up last year. I know she put public records online as part of a preservation project. Come on, let's check."

We scrambled to our feet and asked to use one of the library's computers. Soon we were deep into the history of Easthaven Bay, specifically my bakery.

"Hey, my place used to be a bookstore and supposed smuggling base for rumrunners. So the rumours could be true, and might be a connection to the Johnson and MacNeil families."

"Did the Johnsons own it back then, too?"

"No. It says the owner was an M. LeBlanc."

Hannah gasped. When I stared at her, she squirmed and ducked her head.

Uh, oh. She knows something but doesn't want to tell me.

"Hannah," I tried to be gentle, yet my annoyance slipped out. "What do you know?"

She glanced at me. "That this was probably a bad idea. If M. LeBlanc is who I think it is, then she could have created a concealment spell. She was definitely powerful enough to weave magic that would evade detection from other witches. And if she was involved, then there's a high chance prohibited magic is connected somewhere." Her expression changed to anxiety. "We don't want to be messing with something where she's mixed into it. It could get us banned."

"Who are you talking about?"

"Marie LeBlanc." She said it with fearful reverence, as if it held a dreadful meaning. I was clueless.

"Never heard of her."

"Oh." Hannah blinked and pulled out of her funk. "Yeah, you wouldn't know. Marie LeBlanc was a notorious witch who lived in Easthaven Bay. Rumour had it she emigrated to Canada from New Orleans around 1910. She didn't practice ethical magic, and she was a criminal. A smuggler. She got herself banned from all the local covens and a reputation for selling potions, spells and curses to anyone that would pay. She was accused of murder once, but all the witnesses either mysteriously died, refused to talk or disappeared. She and her grimoire are a local legend to some."

"Grimoire?" My spine prickled. "What happened to that?"

"No one knows. It disappeared after she died. If it even existed."

"Oh, it existed. No witch that powerful would be without a grimoire. In fact, it might be at the center of this whole mess."

"How?"

Ignoring the question I asked, "When did Marie LeBlanc die?"

"Ummm, 1925, I think. Again, under mysterious circumstances. I don't know a lot about her, mostly the older witches telling stories and warning us away."

"Okay, that fits. Let me see…" Some more checking on the computer and I found what I was looking for. "Here. A news article about an explosion on George Johnson's boat. The official cause, a faulty engine. George Johnson was seriously injured, and look, there was one fatality. Marie LeBlanc."

"So they knew each other."

"I bet they were all in cahoots together as they used to say, at least George and Marie. Certainly rum-running criminals. Then Angus MacNeil either double-crossed his partners or tried to eliminate his competitors by sabotaging the boat to kill them."

"And only got one. Why sabotage, though?"

"Money? Or maybe it was all about the grimoire."

"Huh?"

"Think about it. What would be worth killing over? The secret grimoire of a powerful witch. An artifact like that would be sought after by collectors or other witches looking to enhance their abilities. I bet Marie and Johnson died for it, and whoever hired my landlord to snoop around the bakery is after this grimoire. Heck, maybe this mysterious map is the key."

"And no one's located it, map or not, because it's hidden behind that concealment spell." Hannah's face lit up with a grin, seconds before she scowled. "And none of it matters because we can't access the bakery as it's sealed off by the police."

"Neither of those obstacles will stop the person behind this, so we'll have to find some wiggle room. What's the coven policy on recovering illicit magical objects?"

Hannah gave me a funny look, but replied, "Once located or discovered, the object needs to be reported to the Council, which will send out an official retrieval and containment team. Then it's either disposal or long-term containment."

"Good. We haven't broken any rules yet. All this is conjecture, so we can continue to investigate until we find proof. Since we don't know who is involved, I don't want to report to the Council right now."

"Are you sure?" Hannah didn't sound convinced.

"Yes. The only real link we have to Marie LeBlanc is that she once owned my shop. The rest is guesswork. Until we access the shop and uncover the concealment spell, if it exists, we're theorizing. Plus, informing the Council now might alert the killer."

"I suppose. How do we get into the shop with it cordoned off?"

"Good question. The first step is seeing when the police will let me back in, I guess. If it's in a few days, then we can wait. We should go back to my place and make a contingency plan, though."

"Agreed."

We left the library and headed back. Five minutes after arriving, a knock on the front door interrupted and we dashed out to answer it. A gangly kid looked up at us and thrust an envelope at me.

"From Miss Shirley," he said before taking off.

I shut the door and tore open the letter. "It's the list of names." I scanned the paper, Hannah reading over my shoulder. We both gasped at the last name on the list.

Hannah nudged me. "That can't be a coincidence."

"No. And it would explain her persistent interest in me."

Jillian Burke went to the top of the suspect list.

Chapter 7: Arranging Suspects

I made a pot of coffee and dished up some mint chocolate chip ice cream. Then Hannah and I settled on the couch to talk.

"Tell me about Jillian Burke. She moved here last year, right? What's her story? Does she have history with the coven? I've actively avoided her, so all I know is that she's a control freak and has money. Two things I dislike."

"I think it's been more like eighteen months since she moved, but her family does have ties to the town. There were Burkes around Easthaven Bay in the early 1900s; that branch of the family moved away to Halifax in the late 1930s."

"Would they have been here during Marie LeBlanc's time?"

"Yeah. Supposedly they moved to be closer to other relatives. From what I understand, Jillian comes from the original Halifax branch, not the ones that lived in Easthaven Bay."

"So why did she move here? Seems to me she'd be happier in the city than in a rural seaside town. And if she didn't have direct roots, that's even stranger."

"She told everyone she wanted a change, but no one believed her. She never made an effort to fit in and it didn't take long for her to piss people off. Rumours started flying a week after she arrived as to why she moved here, everything from a death in the family, to her being widowed or a messy divorce. No one really knows why she moved..." Hannah frowned. "Come to think of it, she mentioned hearing stories of Easthaven Bay as a child. Said she always wanted to see it for herself."

"That is interesting. I wonder what kind of stories she heard. And I wonder if any of them were about Marie LeBlanc."

"Yeah, it does make you think." Hannah sipped her coffee. "Like how little the coven actually knows about Jillian. I know the Council did a background check, as they do with all new members, so nothing raised any red flags. She doesn't have any close friends in the coven, and as far as I know, doesn't see any of us outside of the meetings."

"What about Emily and Sarah? They did come into the bakery that day, together."

"That must be new, or coven business. They aren't close friends."

"I wonder why they were hanging out then? Anything else?"

"I think Jillian might belong to the Chester Yacht Club, and she makes shopping trips to Halifax all the time."

"Then brags about all the money she spent, I bet."

Hannah giggled. "Yeah. She's conceited, all right."

"Have you seen her hanging out with Johnson?"

Hannah shook her head. "I was surprised she was on the list, that she would hire Johnson for anything magic related. I never thought Jillian was that interested in practicing or studying magic; she acted as if it was more of a status symbol for her." Hannah cleared her throat. "Um, do you think we should be focusing on her? We should probably go over the others as possible suspects too."

"Good point. Just because we don't like someone doesn't mean we should exclude anyone else. You've known these people longer than I have. Does any other name look interesting?"

Hannah glanced down at the list. "Well, we can probably put Nicole and Erin at the bottom of the suspect pool. Nicole collects wands, the older the better; chances are that's why she hired Johnson. And Erin got herself in hot water two years ago over some…erotic items. My guess is that is why she's on the list."

I slurped some coffee to hide my smile.

"The other four are harder to pin down. Laura and Danielle are a bit fickle; they might dabble in the black market to experiment with their magic. Possibly?" Hannah looked at me, expecting my opinion.

"Maybe. I don't know them well. They don't seem like hardened criminal masterminds to me."

"I agree. Emily and Sarah now, we might want to keep an eye on them, and they've been chummy with Jillian too. I know Emily has been at odds with the Council, petitioning to get some of the rules 'modernized' as she put it. She doesn't like some of the restrictions."

"Yeah, I've noticed. She wanted to get me involved a few months ago, but I blew her off. What about Sarah? Why would you suspect her? She's such a quiet woman."

"A quiet woman who loves esoteric research, especially dangerous esoteric research. The Council warned her a couple of times. Something like Marie LeBlanc's grimoire might be catnip for her."

"That would explain her hiring Johnson, I guess, but murder? She seems so sweet."

"You evidently have not been cornered to listen to her talk about her research. That is a side order of slightly unhinged."

"Okay. Sarah and Emily go on the top of the list with Jillian." I paused. "You don't suppose they could be in on it together? The morning before Johnson died, the three of them seemed thick as thieves. And Johnson seemed pretty steamed to see them, too."

"All of them, or one in particular?"

"Good question. He seemed mad at everyone that day, so I can't really say." I thought, picturing the scene. "For whatever it's worth, Emily and Sarah seemed surprised by his reaction, but Jillian didn't bat an eye. My money's still on Jillian being the ringleader."

"Maybe. We can't rule out the others, though, can we?"

I shook my head. "This whole investigation thing sucks. The TV detectives make it look easy."

Hannah laughed. "Don't they just." She scooped up the last of her melting ice cream before continuing. "So what's our next move?"

"Well, we can't investigate the bakery until the police release it, and I think we should be safe in waiting until we get the all-clear. So maybe we should target Emily and Sarah and try to find out what they know."

"Good idea, but we'll need to be subtle about it. I think I know how we can approach Emily. You won't like it."

I took a bite of ice cream and a deep breath. "How?"

"She's having a coven meeting tomorrow for her 'reform movement' as she calls it. We could attend. There's a talk, then food and a mingle after."

Hannah was right. I didn't like it, but it was a sound plan, so I nodded. "That's a good way to see what's going on with her."

"Great. It's tomorrow night at 6 PM in the community centre.

Hannah arrived early for our adventure, and after I answered her knock, she flounced into the house with the dramatic flair of a crime melodrama, exclaiming, "Did you hear? Johnson *was* murdered!"

"Did the police make a statement? Do you know how he died?"

"No official statement yet, but I have a source. It wasn't the infamous fudge. Apparently, when the evidence was analyzed, they found poison in his flask. You know the one he kept tucked in his pocket? Well, that was dosed with cyanide."

"Cyanide? That's good news. It's regulated these days, right? They should be able to trace it and track down the killer. This will be over soon."

"Maybe…" Hannah ducked her head and scuffed her toe on my floor. "Still, it would be dumb for the killer to use something that could be easily traced to them, right? I wouldn't get your hopes up, yet."

"Oh. Wait, do you know something?"

She shrugged. "Nothing definite, but don't count on it being over so soon. In any case, his death will be ruled a homicide, and no official suspects yet."

"How did you find all this out? Isn't it a bit soon for the police to have results?"

"I know, because, well, I talked to Esther. If she says it happened, it happened. Plus, I think they put a rush on the testing. Or maybe it's been slow in the dead body department lately."

"Esther told you? Well, if anyone would have the scoop, it would be her." That woman had relatives all over town. No doubt the information came to Esther through some second cousin twice removed who worked at the police station or the coroner's office.

"Yeah, the woman's uncanny."

I sighed. "Things keep getting worse, don't they? I hope we can dig up some facts at this meeting tonight."

"Should we head over, then? Grill the suspects?"

"Sounds good. Nice outfit, by the way."

"Thanks. You look good too."

I went with a casual chic look, floral skirt and loose shirt, hair pulled back in a ponytail; Hannah chose a bohemian retro dress that matched the pink streak in her hair. Opting to walk through town, we arrived at the community centre about ten minutes before six. As the coven owned and operated the building under the guise of the Easthaven Bay Volunteer Society, members had full private access, which made it ideal for meetings.

As we entered, Hannah leaned over and whispered, "Not much of a turnout."

She was right. Besides the two of us, less than ten people were here, including Emily. I waved to our host, and she bounded over like a homesick puppy.

"Oh, I wasn't expecting you two. Thanks for coming. Especially you, Bridget. I thought you avoided coven politics."

"Yeah, I usually do, but Hannah convinced me I should hear you out. Said you were making some interesting points."

"Oh, wonderful. I am sure you'll enjoy the talk. We have some food and coffee afterward. Not as good as your pastries, though. It's a shame about what happened at the bakery. I hear the police are thinking it's murder? Is that right?"

I nodded.

"Wow. I'm so sorry. Will that keep the bakery closed longer? Do you know when the shop will reopen?"

"Not yet. I'm sure it won't be long." I took a breath and plunged right in. "It's sad and troubling, what happened to Mr. Johnson. I don't even know why he was there that night. He was acting strange that day, though. Even confronted you, Sarah, and Jillian in the shop that morning."

"Oh, that's right. That was odd. Of course, it was probably more for Jillian than Sarah or myself."

"Really?" Inwardly I smiled; she steered the conversation in the perfect direction. "I didn't know they knew each other."

"Oh, yes. Johnson was helping her with some real estate or something. I don't know the details. You know Jillian. Not very talkative about her business. I do think there was friction there, though. I know she wasn't happy with his progress in their venture."

"I didn't realize you and Jillian were that close," Hannah piped into the conversation. "Is she going to be here tonight?"

Emily frowned and curled her lip. "No. I thought she wanted to support the cause, but..." Emily squared her shoulders. "Well, she decided it wasn't worth her time."

That annoyed me. Typical Jillian. Toying with people. "That's her loss."

Emily brightened. "It is. Anyway, thanks for coming. I have to go set up. We'll talk later."

Hannah nudged me. "Emily is looking less like a suspect with Jillian being buddy-buddy with Johnson."

"Yeah. We'd better grab a seat for Emily's talk. I want to stay on her good side so we can find out more."

We settled in a back row, on some uncomfortable folding chairs and listened to Emily and other witches drone on about how the coven was mired in traditional rules and dismissing the needs of younger witches. It wasn't anything I hadn't heard before in Toronto, yet Emily did have some innovative suggestions for change. I might have been too quick to dismiss her concerns and cause.

As we rose, I noticed Sarah heading to the buffet table. "Sarah's here. We should talk to her." Hannah trailed after me as I made a beeline to the other witch.

I subtly bumped her as we both reached for a roll. "Oh, sorry."

Sarah looked up startled, then relaxed. "Bridget, it's you."

"Expecting someone else?"

"No, no. I'm on edge, I guess."

"Yeah, me too. This whole thing with Johnson. So awful."

"Yes, you poor thing." She paused, her mouth thin, before blurting, "Um, have you heard anything? About the investigation? I mean have the police…are they looking into his businesses?"

My ears pricked up. "They haven't told me anything. Were you in business with him too? I know he was…freelancing with some of the coven witches."

"There were others? Oh, dear. I hope these things don't come out. It might be embarrassing."

"I wouldn't think the police would be interested, unless it was criminal or something."

"Oh no, nothing like that. It's just…" Sarah bit her lip.

"It's all right. I know how restrictive coven rules can be. That's why we're all here tonight, right? Because we want change?"

"Oh, I'm so glad you understand." Sarah touched my arm. "With your heritage, I thought you'd be, well, very in line with things."

I shook my head. "I've seen enough reactive policies to last a lifetime. My whole childhood was living up to the coven ideal. You need some rules, of course, but things ought to be more flexible, don't you think? More individual?"

"Exactly. Then witches wouldn't have to turn to people like Mr. Johnson."

"Yes." I moved in with the sympathy ploy. "He wasn't very nice to work with, was he? I had quite a bit of trouble with him as a landlord."

"The man was horrid. I can't say I'm sorry he's dead." She gasped a little. "Oh, that sounded dreadful. It's just…" She hesitated then said, "I had him acquire something for me that the Council wouldn't like. Nothing dangerous, still… Mr. Johnson wasn't a nice man. He tried to…" She leaned in and whispered, "*Blackmail* me."

"What?" I was honestly shocked. "That's disgusting."

"Don't worry, I showed him. Threatened to give him boils. On his, well…" She blushed and glanced downward.

I got the gist and smiled. "Served him right."

Before I could wheedle more information, someone waved at Sarah and she moved to join her friends.

I turned to Hannah. "Did you hear all that?"

She nodded. "Puts a new spin on things. I wonder if Johnson was blackmailing anyone else?"

"And whether that was the motive for killing him? I think we need to have a long chat with our ghost."

"Do you mean?"

"I do. It's time to hold a summoning."

Chapter 8: Ghosts and Grimoires

The next evening Hannah and I were in the living room prepared to summon a ghost. We pushed back the furniture, sketched the summoning circle and the runic protection symbols on the floor with washable chalk, and placed the candles. I stood outside the circle, ready with the incantation, as Hannah lit the candles. When the last flame flickered into life, Hannah stepped back to join me and I recited the spell.

"Arise, afflicted spirit. Arise and show yourself. Arise and speak to us."

Violet energy illuminated the summoning ring, moving along the enclosed line in a clockwise direction, and the protection symbols glowed an eerie diaphanous green. The temperature in the room dropped and the air vibrated with a soft humming noise.

Louder, I repeated, "Arise, afflicted spirit. Arise and show yourself. Arise and speak to us."

Grey mist oozed up from the floor, filling the circle, the lights flickered on the walls, and the candle flames waved in an invisible breeze. A wailing moan broke the silence as the mist swirled and surged, transforming into a gossamer form.

As it took shape, the ghost of Jeffery Johnson floated in the center of the circle.

"It worked!" Hannah bounced on her toes beside me. I ignored her antics.

Taking a deep breath, I blurted, "Jeffery Johnson, tell us who killed you."

The ghost wavered, the edges of its ephemeral vapours shifting, unable to fade out, caught in the circle's power. He moaned, finally focusing on Hannah and myself.

I repeated the question, "Jeffery Johnson, tell us who killed you."

"Witch, witch, witch!" The shriek spooked an irritated Taffy, who hissed, pawed at the floor, and then took off at a run.

"Who? I want a name!"

Johnson's ghost opened its mouth but no sound came out. It shook its head and whispered, "Witch."

Hannah nudged me. "What's going on?"

"I don't think the ghost can tell us. A spell maybe, or a compulsion, is preventing it." I frowned. "Let's try something else. Why were you murdered?"

"Found something. Knew…how…double-cross…"

"Your partner double-crossed you?" Hannah's excited voice broke into the conversation.

"No. Wanted…grimoire. Hidden… bakery…didn't want to share."

Hannah and I exchanged looks. I whispered, "Jillian."

That agitated the ghost.

"She didn't want…not after grim…wanted…" The ghost wavered and then as clear as a bell shrieked, "Amber!" He flickered out before returning and whispering, "Gave me…never trusted…I died. Killed me!"

His last two words shook through our bones and the lights flickered in the room. He howled and a gust of wind swirled inside the circle snuffing out the candles one by one. In a flash of emerald radiance, the ghost was gone.

Hannah's shoulders slumped. "Poor Mr. Johnson."

"Yeah, I guess."

"You guess? The man was murdered by some rogue witch and is now trapped as a ghost."

"True, but it sounded like he also conspired with a witch to unearth a powerful grimoire. Probably for money. Maybe he had second thoughts, yet he might have double-crossed his partner. And if his tactics with Sarah are any indication, maybe he tried blackmail too. Johnson might have gotten screwed, and he didn't deserve to be killed, but he put himself in the situation." I sighed. "And dragged us into it as well."

"I suppose. I still feel sorry for him." Hannah walked over to the moved sofa and flopped down. "This whole summoning was a bust. We didn't learn anything new."

I sat beside her. "No, but we confirmed what we suspected. And I think we can concentrate on Jillian. Johnson established she's part of this. That she wanted amber for some reason? Why would she need Johnson for that? It's a common spell ingredient."

Hannah shook her head. "No clue. Maybe Marie had some special variety."

"I guess. It's odd, though."

"Another mystery." Hannah huffed. "We need to get into the bakery! When do you think the police will release the crime scene?"

"I'll give them a call tomorrow." I leaned back into the cushions. "In the meantime, let's drown our frustrations in ice cream, then clean up this mess." I waved my hand at the defunct chalk circle and snuffed out candles.

"Sounds like a plan. Rocky Road or mint chocolate chip?"

I called the police the next morning and was dutifully informed that my bakery would be released sometime that day and to wait for the call. Since Hannah had to work, I binge watched some shows, surrounded by my magic books, old study journals and my grimoire, obsessing over the mystery. I researched concealment spells, specifically detecting and breaking them, jotting down useful notes. I also dug into spell lore, but couldn't find any mention of special varieties of amber.

Maybe this is all about Marie's grimoire? We need to find it.

It all came down to that. And what to do with it if I found it? I wasn't keen to turn it over to the Council; that might make it easier for Jillian to steal it. I also wasn't keen on keeping the thing and possibly getting reprimanded.

I guess I can decide if and when we ever locate it.

The police called me in the afternoon, after I took a deserved break from research, informing me the bakery had been released as a crime scene, and gave me a number for a good cleaning service, something I hadn't thought of.

Another problem.

I called Hannah who agreed to meet me at the bakery in an hour after her shift, and then phoned the cleaning service. They agreed to fit me in within two days and I scheduled an appointment. I printed off a quick re-opening sign and sped off to the bakery with a bag full of supplies and research material.

After unlocking the door, I stood there, waiting to go in. Flashes of memory swirled, of Johnson lying on my kitchen floor, the panicked feeling, the police. My cozy shop seemed almost tainted now.

I can't let this ruin everything. This is still my bakery, my dream.

So, with a few breaths to calm my nerves, I walked into my bakery. No ghosts popped up, no dead bodies; only the familiar sights and smells, even if the air was a bit stale. I could do this. I could figure all this out.

I taped the sign on the front door, informing customers the bakery would reopen next week. I figured that would give me enough time to get the place clean and everything restocked. Everything still in the fridge would be stale or useless; I might be able to salvage some of it by selling it on discount, but most of it would go into my home freezer, home with my employees, or to the food bank.

I headed to the kitchen first, surveying the mess the police left behind, which was minor, and then checked the fridge. Nothing was spoiled or moldy, only wilted and stodgy. Nobody would want to buy cakes with sagging whipped cream or slightly soggy pastries. I made a note of what I could drop off at the soup kitchen, what I could freeze for personal use or send home with my employees, and what might last another day or two. It wouldn't hurt to leave the cleaning crew free treats.

Donning a mask and gloves, I did some quick tidying: boxing sweets, some dusting, disposing of fudge remnants, wiping down the counters to keep busy while I waited for Hannah. I wasn't too worried about leaving the deep cleaning for the professionals; the bakery was spelled against bugs and vermin.

After finishing my cursory cleaning, I did check by the back door to see if I could sense anything, but I didn't find a trace of magic. At least not concealment magic from a 1920s witch. Outside, I could sense a more recent presence with the whiff of a contemporary rich witch.

Jillian Burke snuck around my shop.

The bell at the front door signalled Hannah's arrival and I dashed out to greet her.

"You're opening next week? That's great. Find anything yet?"

"Traces of Jillian sneaking around outside." I clicked the lock on the door so we wouldn't have any unwanted interruptions. "No trace of the other spell, though. Not that I expected any. We are definitely going to have to force a revelation of sorts."

I followed Hannah into the back of the shop.

"What's the plan?"

"Oh, shoot. Just a sec." I raced back to the shop front and retrieved the copies of the spell I worked up and the other components. Returning to Hannah, I handed her a copy. "This modified revealing spell will hopefully do the trick."

"Are you sure? This is a powerful spell. Are we strong enough to reverse it?"

"We aren't trying to reverse it, only see what's hidden. As long as the magic connects, it should unravel the spell, at least for us. If we don't attempt to break the spell, only expose it, even magic this powerful should bend."

"Okay. Let's try it."

While Hannah familiarized herself with the spell, I placed three white candles in a triangle shape in front of where I estimated the alcove to be located, before sprinkling a circle of specially blended herbs around the candles. I lit the candles and watched the flames flicker evenly.

"Okay, everything's ready. Are you good to go?"

"Yeah, it's an excellent adaptation of a standard reveal spell. Love the extra kick you added. Great spellwork."

"Say that after it works."

Hannah laughed.

"Are you clear on your part?"

She nodded and then we began.

I cleared my throat and intoned, "Power of the flame, burn away the fabrication, sweep away layers of illusion and reveal what was once clear."

The fire of the candles flared and the smell of lavender and thyme infused into the room.

"Release the knowledge from the past," Hannah added her voice to the spell. "Uncover the hidden, liberate the memory of disguise and disclose what dwells beyond false sight."

Again the candles flared, but this time the aroma of rosemary and nutmeg filled the room.

Hannah and I recited together, "For the sake of truth, and a soul's true rest, we entreat to disrupt the binding, we invoke protection against the dark secrets and a witch's power, we ask now, reveal the reality here, the nature of what was concealed, and push back the shadows into the light!"

The candle flames burst upward in a surge of energy and the room saturated with the smell of dill and lemony vervain, the last ingredients in the spell. We held our breath, afraid for a moment the spell failed, before the air beyond the candles slowly shimmered and shifted, revealing a translucent curtain of energy.

Stepping carefully around the candles, Hannah and I approached the magical screen. I gingerly reached out a hand and touched a fingertip to the barrier. It dissolved in a flash of light, exposing a tiny alcove and an iron-wrought, spiral staircase.

"It worked!" Hannah clapped her hands. "Where does that go?" She waved at the stairs.

"Only one way to find out." I grabbed the railing and climbed; Hannah's footsteps right behind me.

We climbed past the second floor of the building, which was a surprise, because as far as I knew there wasn't a third storey to this building. The bakery took up the first level, and I used some of the second storey for storage and an employee bathroom, but there wasn't supposed to be a third floor. The fact that the concealment spell encompassed an entire floor, to the point it wasn't even visible on the outside, amazed and frightened me. A witch that could create something like that was on par with or stronger than my mother.

The stairs rose up to a hidden third floor, to what I assumed was the building's attic. Hannah and I emerged into a spacious furnished room, sunlight streaming in from a street-facing cupola window. Glancing around, I saw a desk, a bed, tables, and cupboards. There wasn't much headroom, but enough so we wouldn't be banging our skulls on the rafters. I lingered at the staircase entrance, as Hannah walked around staring at everything.

"I can't believe this was here the whole time. Hidden from the entire town. This isn't some secreted door and cubbyhole; it's a complete freaking garret."

"Yeah. My question is why."

"It's fairly obvious, isn't it? This was Marie LeBlanc's sanctuary. Where she created her spells and potions and who knows what else. We are standing inside Easthaven Bay witch history." She twirled, her voice full of awe.

I smiled. Hannah loved history so much.

"Yeah, I'm sure this was her sanctuary, but why conceal it? She wasn't hiding her activities from the witch community and a simple repulsion spell on the staircase would have kept out the non-witches. Heck, most witches too, if she worded it right."

Hannah frowned. "Maybe she was afraid of something?"

I shivered. What could make a powerful witch like her afraid? "That's a sobering thought."

"Yeah, she was murdered after all. Well, probably murdered. Maybe the boat explosion wasn't the first attempt."

Hannah could be right. "We should look for any journals, too, while we search for the grimoire. If she kept any, they might give us answers."

Hannah nodded and we set to work ransacking the room. Most of the cabinets and cupboards held brittle spell ingredients and dried-up potions, plus a few amulets, trinkets, and some esoteric stuff we were afraid to touch. Yet no grimoire, not even a page or two of handwritten incantations.

"Marie wasn't one to leave her spells lying around, was she? A careful witch, our Marie." I huffed. "Let's try her desk."

Searching, we found the desk drawers empty until the last one on the right. There we discovered a thick diary of sorts, full of spell notations, and observations of Easthaven Bay in the 20s.

"Doesn't look too earth-shattering," Hannah remarked, "but we'd best read it to find out."

"Maybe it'll have a clue to what happened back then, give us an idea of what happened to her missing grimoire." I flopped down in a creaky chair and immediately coughed on the dust. "It doesn't look like she hid it here."

"Yeah," Hannah agreed. "Which is odd. If the grimoire isn't here, if nothing important is here, then like you said, why hide the place? It doesn't make sense."

"We must be missing something. And I'm hungry. Let's go downstairs and eat some stale pastry or something. Read that book and get some context or clues."

"Will we be able to return? Find this place again?"

"We should. The spell we wove will hide the entrance from the rest of the world while allowing us to see it."

Hannah's expression looked dubious. "I think I'll stay here. Read the journal. Look around some more. You go eat something. That way we'll have two perspectives mulling this over."

I shrugged. "Okay. Do you want me to bring you a snack?"

She shook her head and flipped open the book. "Hey, there's an old photo in here. Take a look." She held up a sepia snapshot of three people, two men and one woman standing in front of the bakery building. The third floor could be seen clearly.

"Hey, I bet that's Marie, Angus and George."

"I bet you're right." Hannah tucked the photo back in the diary and started reading.

I knew I lost her attention so I descended the stairs, moving to the kitchen. I munched down on a limp eclair and a stale maple croissant, mulling over the problem.

How could I stop one rogue witch from targeting my bakery in a mad attempt to find another rogue witch's grimoire? Not to mention that she may have poisoned someone for getting in her way. What would she do to us?

I don't need this trouble.

I thought these types of problems were behind me. Dealing with drama and conniving witches, in-fighting, and backstabbing coven politics was why I left Toronto and moved here. Back there I was always cleaning up other people's messes; it was expected of me as Vivian Redwood's daughter. At least, that's what my mother expected.

Leave it to me to rent the old hangout of a rum-running 1920s villainous witch. Where did you hide the grimoire, Marie? And why? I bet you liked to play games, like my mother.

That was a thought. What would the great Vivian Redwood do if she needed to hide something from her enemies? I closed my eyes and channeled my mother. What would she do? Would she create… It hit me. She would flaunt it. Hide it in plain sight. Another concealment spell? No, that would have broken with the first one. Maybe a disguise?

"Bridget! I found something!"

Hannah's yell broke my chain of thought and I dashed back up to the hidden attic. Hannah was sitting in the desk chair and waved the journal at me as I climbed back into the room.

"Marie was at odds with Angus MacNeil. Listen." Hannah read a passage from the journal.

Why did that dratted Angus MacNeil pull a double-cross now? He was fine with smuggling bootleg hooch and supplying those high-hat coven dames with their trinkets, but he gets cold feet at expanding the operation? Coward. Can't handle me calling all the shots or messing with this rinky-dink village. No, over that he gets a case of the heebie-jeebies. Tells me he's out, then goes and pinches the fire amber. Hides it somewhere. Too bad George couldn't get his hands on that map. I can get more amber, but it'll put the plan back weeks. And now MacNeil wants to get his grubby hands on my grimoire! Jokes on him. George and me are heading out of this backwater to lay low and he'll never find it. I'll deal with MacNeil when I get back.

Hannah closed the journal. "Sounds like Angus Macneil opposed one of Marie's plans, something big. Maybe that's why he caused the boat to explode."

"Could be, and it may answer why she hid this room. She was leaving town and didn't want Angus or anyone else snooping around."

"You think this fire amber is what Johnson mentioned, what he was looking for? Not the grimoire or this room?"

"Maybe. Fire amber sounds familiar. Not sure where I heard the name, though. Does the diary say anything more about it?"

"Not that I read, and I've never heard of it."

"Maybe it'll come to me."

"I hope so. We could use some insight."

I nodded. "Might explain the map, too. Maybe it is a treasure map, and it points to this amber, the location of what Angus stole."

"The journal could explain where the grimoire is as well." Hannah sighed.

"Why would you say that?"

"Marie was leaving. She probably had the grimoire with her on the boat. That book is probably at the bottom of the harbour."

"Unless she hid it. The journal says she was coming back." I puffed out my chest a little. "I had a bit of a breakthrough too. Maybe. I think Marie's grimoire is still here."

"Really? Where? How do we find it?"

"We'll need a few things. Did you see any candles here earlier?

"Yeah, the corner cupboard had a stash. Some white ones, a few red, black ones, and some blue ones."

"Good. Dig out the blue and white ones and set up a candle circle in the center of the room. Marie already has a conjuring space set up there." I nodded at the runes etched into the floor. "I'm going to pop out and pick up the other things we need."

I climbed back downstairs and exited out the back door, headed to my house. Once there, I loaded up on supplies, slid everything into a reusable bag and went back to the bakery and the attic. Hannah had arranged the candles perfectly and I set up the crystals and rune stones that we needed for the spell.

"A scrying spell? That's a bit iffy without knowing exactly what we're looking for."

"Not exactly a scrying spell. It's similar, but it's specialized; there's a bit of a revelation spell mixed in."

"Huh? What are you thinking?"

"Marie was clever, sneaky, and liked to flaunt it. I'm thinking the grimoire is here somewhere, disguised as something else. This spell, hopefully, will pierce the disguise."

Hannah stepped back and let me work. I lit the candles, watching curls of smoke drift towards the ceiling. I felt the pulse of the crystals and the runes catch the warmth of the flames, and then recited the spell.

"Candle, Crystal, and Rune show us what we seek. Candle, Crystal, and Rune, reveal the secrets hidden. Candle, Crystal, and Rune, unveil the invisible."

A hum filled the room as the spell spiralled through its working. The cupboards rattled in sympathetic harmony with the sound, clinking the potion bottles inside, and the floorboards vibrated under my feet. I let the magic wash over me until a trickle of light spun out of the center of the circle and floated past my ear. I turned and watched the thread weave itself around a thick book tucked into a bookshelf above the desk.

A burst of red energy flashed, revealing Marie LeBlanc's grimoire. A brief scent of jasmine filled the air.

"Is that it?" Hannah rushed forward, tracing a finger along the gilded edge. "It is the grimoire. I can feel the power emanating from it." She withdrew her hand and took a step back, shivering.

Hannah was right. I felt its energy from where I stood, now that its disguise was gone. The grimoire radiated dark power, something I hadn't messed with since I was a teenager; memories of that illicit dalliance washed over me.

Studying the large book, I saw it was in flawless condition, bound in brown leather with gilt edging, with a soft purple undertone that glowed. A palpable magic overflowed into the room, and settled across my skin with a strange warmth. I heard the soft strains of jazz, and the scent of magnolia and lemon swirled around me like a familiar blanket.

I felt a siren's call pulling me towards the book and shook my head to disrupt the sensations.

This isn't good.

I turned around and blew out the candles.

"Hey! It's gone, I mean it looks like the old book again. Why did you do that?"

I ignored her while I dismantled the spell circle, tucking my crystals and runes in their bag and returning the candles to the cupboard. Then I answered Hannah.

"Do you really want to erect a signpost for Jillian saying here it is, come get the grimoire? You felt the power when it revealed itself. Can you feel anything now?"

"No." Hannah looked at me. "I don't."

"Yeah. Marie hid her grimoire very well, and I think it is best for it to remain that way for now."

"Are we going to leave it here? Not tell anyone?"

"Yes and no. We are not going to tell anyone yet, because we don't know who to trust. Jillian's involved to be sure, but we have no proof to take to the Council. And can we be certain she's working alone?"

"I guess not. Still, it's a risk. We could get in trouble for not reporting this."

"All the more reason for leaving the grimoire's disguise in place. We can claim that all we did was remove a reference book from a hidden witch's sanctuary." I strode over and picked up the grimoire. It didn't even tingle in my arms and I sighed in relief. "See, anyone who sees it will think it's a copy of *Alfson's Guide To Runic Spellcasting and Divination.*

"So, we are taking it with us?"

"Yes." I slid another sack out of my supply bag and placed the grimoire inside, out of sight.

Hannah moved closer. "Are you sure? This seems underhanded. The Council should be told."

"They will be, but not now. Not until we know who is involved." I laid a reassuring hand on her arm. "For now, let's get out of here."

She frowned at me, but nodded.

We descended to the bakery and retrieved the candles used in the concealment spell and swept up the mess of herbs. The staircase was still visible to both of us after we dismantled the spell.

"See, nothing to worry about. We can get back to the room any time we want."

Hannah nodded in relief and we moved to the kitchen. I collected the boxes I wanted to drop off at the soup kitchen and what I would take home, putting more boxes in the bakery's freezer. Then we left.

Neither Hannah nor I felt like talking after finding the grimoire; the significance of what we were doing weighed on both of us. After the soup kitchen, we both went our separate ways. I made it home safely, resisting the urge to look over my shoulder every five minutes to see if I was being followed.

I tucked the stale pastries in the freezer and went upstairs with Marie's book. I sat on the edge of the bed with the wrapped book in my lap. Curiosity got the best of me and I slid the book out to take a closer look.

The disguise spellwork was magnificent; the texture of the grimoire felt like a hardcover, not a leather-bound book, and the look of it didn't shimmer or waver, not even when I flipped through the pages. The smell of it was even perfect, giving off that old book scent.

"You were good, Marie. On par with Mother. What secrets does this book hold, I wonder?"

My fingers itched to unlock it and take a peek, but I yielded to good sense and placed it back in the bag.

"What am I going to do with you?"

I glanced at the closet. It should be safe enough there. The disguise was flawless. Placing the book on the bed, I went and made some room on the top shelf. Then I tucked the bag holding the grimoire in the new space. Taking the time to create a quick hex bag as a booby trap and warning system, I inserted that beside the book, before returning downstairs. Then I got myself a large glass of wine and flopped on the couch. I raised it and toasted my dead landlord.

"Thanks, Mr. Johnson, for bringing this trouble right to my doorstep."

"I'm sorry."

I nearly choked on my wine and had to catch myself from spilling the glass over the couch. I shivered in the suddenly frigid air and watched my ghost materialize in front of me.

"Well, you should be sorry. Dragging me into this sordid mess." I glared, noticing he was a bit more coherent and stable. That happened sometimes with ghosts when their anchor got stronger; I guess my summoning strengthened him. Didn't mean I had to like his popping in, though.

"Are you happy now? I'm stuck cleaning up the trouble you caused. What were you thinking? Smuggling contraband for witches was one thing, but being Jillian Burke's henchman? That was low, even for you."

"Good money. Didn't know." The familiar whine of Johnson stayed with him in death.

"Really? It was greed? Tell me you at least wanted to be Jillian's partner or something? Hanky panky on the side?"

Hanky panky? I must be spending too much time in Marie LeBlanc's head.

Johnson shook his head. "Thought she…was nuts. Took money…didn't believe her. At first."

"Then it was too late." I sipped wine to drown my annoyance. "What did you do to get her angry enough to kill you? Was it blackmail? Sarah said you tried that on her."

The ghost tried to speak, wildly shaking his head, sputtering gibberish, before finally spitting out, "Wanted…last big payday. Mistake."

"Yeah. A huge mistake." I swirled my wine, watching the crimson liquid dance circles inside the glass. "Women like Jillian don't care about people. They'll hurt anyone, destroy anyone that gets in their way." I looked up at the ghost with pity. "You tried to play in her league and paid the price. You might not have been the best of people, but you didn't deserve that."

A moan escaped the ghost and its form shivered. With one last, "No, no… I'm sorry…" my personal phantom faded away, leaving me depressed. I finished off the wine and went to the kitchen to pour another glass. On my way back to the couch someone knocked at the door.

Part of me wanted to ignore it and hoped they would leave, but the stupid, more practical part made me open the door.

It was Jack.

"You found the hidden room, didn't you?"

Chapter 9: Tidbits

I stared, anger staining the edges of my drunken buzz and sour mood. "Get inside. And you better have a good explanation for what you said." I grabbed his arm and yanked him inside, meeting no resistance. Slamming the door, I led him into the living room, where he settled onto the couch.

I glared at him. "You better not be working for Jillian!"

"What? No. How— Why do you think she's involved in this?"

"She's the one looking for..." *I better be careful. I almost said the "G" word.* "... Something in my bakery. Presumably this hidden room. She hired Johnson to snoop around for it. She could have murdered him, too."

I glared again, and set down the wine glass I still held. "Now tell me, how are *you* involved?" I flopped in a chair, still scowling.

He didn't answer. "Interesting. I knew Johnson was after something when he came sniffing around for my map. I never suspected Jillian, but I assumed someone in the coven was behind his sudden interest."

Oh, I forgot about the map.

I leaned forward. "Answer my question or get out. I'm knee-deep in a mess thanks to Jillian and Johnson's ghost and you're going to tell me what you know."

"Johnson's ghost? You're being haunted? Did the ghost tell you? Is that why you went looking for the room?"

I nodded, letting him believe his assumptions. "Tell me how you knew about it?"

He evaded the question again. "What did you find there?"

Fishing for the grimoire? I wasn't going to bite. "Only dried up potions and a journal. Marie LeBlanc didn't like you great-whatever grandfather, I can tell you. Accused him of double-crossing her and stealing from her." Then, I dropped a bombshell. "Pretty sure Angus MacNeil murdered her too."

"That's not true! Not murder. He was protecting people." Jack's face went red, his voice angry, his whole demeanour flustered. That was the first time I'd seen him without his self-assured confidence.

"I mean, he rigged the explosion to stop her from upsetting the balance, from destroying the town." He dipped his head, staring at his toes. "He wasn't a murderer. It was the only way to prevent her plan."

"You still haven't answered my question. How do you know about Marie and what's your connection to Johnson?"

Jack pressed his lips together and swallowed. "Marie has been family lore forever. Stories about her go back a couple of generations. You're right about Angus stealing from Marie; he took some magical artifact to prevent her schemes. When Johnson came looking to buy Angus' map, I became suspicious of his motives. That's why we were at odds."

"What about the map? What is it?"

"I don't know exactly. The family story says the map is a connection to what was stolen, but it's never been deciphered. It's not even a map, really, not in the traditional sense; what's written on it is a bunch of gibberish."

I sat up straight. "What kind of gibberish?"

"Squiggly nonsense runes mostly."

Was everything involved with Marie disguised or hidden? These people must have been seriously paranoid to have this level of secrecy. Still…

"It might not be gibberish." Jack waited for more but I didn't elaborate, only asked, "Tell me everything you know about Marie's secret room."

He scowled, yet this time he gave me an answer. "The MacNeils have been keeping an eye on her old place of business—your bakery—for decades. The story of her sanctuary and its mysterious disappearing act has been a long-time family secret. My father put a few magical, well, sensors for a lack of a better word, around the place a few years ago. They were tripped today."

"You bugged my bakery!" I stared in outrage. "How did I not sense that!"

Was I going soft? Losing my edge?

"Don't take it personally. That's Dad's specialty, sneaking his magic under a witch's radar. Plus, he installed the spells before you bought the place."

A lot of magic is happening under my radar. Maybe I am going soft.

I took a breath and calmed down. "Okay, that explains that, but I'm not happy. I want those 'sensors' removed."

Jack nodded.

"Now, tell me about Angus and the map. I'm not surprised you can't read it. Marie's journal suggested everyone was keeping secrets. Do you know what Angus stole?"

Jack took a deep breath and leaned forward. "Okay. I'm trusting you with this. How much is true, I'm not sure. None of this was written down or anything. It's all been passed down from generation to generation. Angus MacNeil was a rumrunner and well, a bit of a scoundrel. Nothing serious, until he got mixed up with George Johnson and Marie LeBlanc."

"What were those three up to?"

"They met through coven connections; our family used to be respected members." Jack grimaced. "Initially, they were rum-running, and doing some artifact smuggling on the side for witches."

Well, apparently that still runs in the Johnson family.

"Marie was also trading potions and spells in the States during their trips. I think that's when she discovered it."

"What?"

"That we don't know, exactly. It was some big spell, something powerful, prohibited. Marie was obsessed with it, trying to figure out how to use it to her benefit. That's when Angus turned on her, tried to stop her by stealing…something. In the end, he killed her. And that got the family kicked out of the coven."

"You don't know what he stole?"

Jack shook his head. "All we know is the old map was part of it. A record of something." He shrugged. "Maybe where he hid what he took from Marie."

So Angus never mentioned the fire amber. And why does that still sound so familiar?

"You're right about it being a magical artifact or ingredient." Now it was my turn to take a breath and trust Jack. "Do you know what fire amber is?"

He shook his head. "Never heard of it."

"I recognize the name, but I can't remember where or how. I wish I could."

"Is there anyone you could ask?"

There was, but calling Mother might be stirring up even more trouble. She'd want to know what I was messing with and if it turned out to be a prohibited substance like I suspected, she'd send someone to intervene. I shook my head.

Jack gave me a skeptical look, but said nothing. I took a sip of wine and tried not to squirm. Luckily a knock at the front door interrupted the awkward moment.

I jumped up. "Stay here until I get rid of whoever is at the door."

Hurrying out of the living room, I glanced back as I reached the hall. Of course, Jack didn't listen and followed me.

Why do men have to be so obstinate?

I flung open the door. Jillian stood on my front doorstep.

She smiled at me, a half smirk, half insincere falsehood, and wholly irritating. "Am I interrupting something?" She nodded at Jack, her tone suggestive.

"No," I snapped, hoping I wasn't blushing. "What can I do for you?"

"Oh, I came to see how you are doing after the awful tragedy in your shop."

She pushed her way inside, literally shoving me out of the way, only stopping when Jack presented a bigger obstacle to her entry.

"Such a horrible thing, isn't it Bridget, dear, Johnson dying in your bakery. And so very sordid, turning out to be a murder. Who could do such a thing to you, poisoning your landlord in your place of business? That makes you the prime suspect."

Is that what you planned?

I wanted to smack the smug expression off her face. I scowled, replying, "Yes, it is very tragic that a man was killed, but the suspect pool is wide open. The poison was in his flask. Anyone he knew could have added it." I glared at her.

"What?" Jillian looked genuinely shocked. "How do you know that?"

"I have my sources." It was my turn to look smug.

In a minute her composed mask was back in place. "Well, that's good news. You won't be the main suspect then?"

Sorry your plans got ruined.

"Yes, the police have moved on. I hope they catch the murderer quickly." I moved to her side and put my hand on her arm. "Thanks for coming over, but you can see I'm fine." I tightened my grip and forced her towards the open door, out of my house.

"Well, goodbye then. If you need anything, let me know."

"Of course," I said with a fake smile and shut the door in her face.

"What was that all about?" Jack moved closer.

"Not sure. Maybe Jillian was trying to rub it in, or maybe she was fishing for info."

"Was it wise to tell her that you're not a suspect?"

"It's probably all over town by now. My information 'source' was Esther."

"Still, I'd be careful around her. If she did murder Johnson, she's dangerous. And she may have tried to set you up, Bridget."

"I'm betting that had more to do with keeping me occupied so she could search my shop, than any personal vendetta."

"Still, if she thinks you're a threat, she'll come after you. Be careful."

"Which is why we need to work together and figure out what she wants. What she's up to." I took a deep breath, and asked, "Will you bring me the map so I can take a look at it?"

Jack ran his hands through his hair and avoided looking at me.

"It's important, Jack. I know this is your family history, but someone got killed over this. Heck, more than one someone, if you count Marie. I think I can help solve the mystery."

Jack sighed. "All right, but not tonight. I have a family dinner later, and a shift at the bar after. I'll meet you back here in the morning." He brushed past me and out the door.

Chapter 10: Examination

The next day, I paced nervously in the hall waiting for Jack, nearly jumping when the knock on the door sounded. I flung open the door, and ushered Jack inside, checking the street to make sure there was no sign of anyone watching.

Oh great, the paranoia is catching.

"Did you bring it?"

He nodded and pulled a weathered scrolled piece of paper from under his jacket. "Here it is."

"Bring it into the kitchen. I made coffee."

I poured two cups and Jack unrolled his map on the kitchen table. It wasn't big but was in remarkably good condition for a century-old map; I could feel the magic embedded in the paper. I sipped my coffee, studying what was written on the parchment. Jack told the truth when he said it was nothing but scribbled runes. He was wrong about it being gibberish.

"I think this is the Theban alphabet, maybe a variant of some kind. Some of it I can decipher, but other parts..." I frowned, trying to determine if the squiggles were an altered form of the alphabet or bad handwriting.

"What does it say? I mean the parts you can translate." Jack leaned in eagerly, his face inches from mine.

I ducked my head to hide a blush and tried to concentrate on the words. "This spells Main Street, I think. And the rest..." I frowned, biting my lip. "Maybe it's, 'go to Main Street at the' ...what is that word? Stats, no statue maybe?"

"The town square statue!" Jack's excited voice made me jump. "It's been there since 1910, I think. It was certainly standing in Angus' day. Do you think that's where he hid it, whatever it is that he stole?"

"Maybe. With these words, it's hard to tell if I'm translating it properly. I don't know if Angus changed the alphabet or had atrocious handwriting. Hang on a minute." I jumped up and rummaged for a pad and pen before returning.

"Okay, so we have Main Street and statue." I wrote that down and turned back to the map. "I think that word is 'see' and that one is 'truth'." I jotted down more notes. "Maybe 'spell' for this one." I sighed and put down the pen. "I think he's used different variants to write this. I'm not sure I can translate this without some help. I need a research book." I leaned back and rubbed my neck. "Maybe Hannah can find what I need in the coven archives, but that might be a longshot."

"And what do you need?"

"*The Study of the Runes of Honorius* by A. M. Gatts. It's an obscure study of Theban alphabet and its variants used by various covens through the years. I read it during my magic studies, but I don't own a copy."

Jack cleared his throat. "I have a copy of that book. Um, inherited from my grandfather. It's tucked away in a trunk."

"Really? I wonder if your grandfather got it from Angus. Could be why this 'map' is written in Theban." I stood. "Can you bring over the book? It could be the key."

"Why don't you come over to the house? It's only a short walk."

I hesitated, feeling uneasy. Did I want to go to his house? Isn't he kind of a suspect?

But it's Jack. What did I think would happen?

Still. "Sure, but let me text Hannah. She said she might come over later." Not true, but at least someone would know where I was. I sent her a text message, and then we left.

A short stroll later we arrived at Jack's house; I waved at his nosy neighbour, Mrs. Boyd, as we entered. Another witness, in case.

In case of what? I think paranoia is catching.

Jack's place was an older home, with a red and white exterior, and a neatly kept yard. A typical house in Easthaven Bay. Upon entering, the interior gave off austere vibes, with soft warm colours and minimal decor. As I followed Jack, I walked past bare walls and no clutter; the opposite of my own home.

Settling on the sofa in his living room, I noticed a few personal items like photos, a couple of knickknacks, a sports trophy, and not much else. The place felt unlived in.

"Wait here, I'll go get the book."

Jack left, and I heard him climb the stairs. A picture on the far wall caught my attention, an old sepia photograph of Easthaven Bay. A snapshot of Main Street, and the scene hadn't changed much over the years. A few different buildings nowadays, like the fast-food restaurant and the gift shop, but the landmarks, the clocktower and the town hall, were practically unchanged.

I wonder if that photo is from the 1920s?

"I found it!" Jack bounded into the room with a grin plastered on his face and dropped the book in my lap. I settled in, going through the pages, consulting the notes I'd made and the map, slowly checking bits of the text for the right translation. I considered the different alphabets, different combinations, until finally finding a few possible options. "Here, I think this may be what Angus—"

A knock on Jack's front door interrupted, and he jumped up to answer it. Curious, I watched from the sofa as he opened the door. The police were waiting on the other side.

"Jack MacNeil, we need you to come with us. We have some questions regarding the death of Jeffery Johnson."

I quietly shut the book, rolled the map, and moved to the door with both items and my notes. "What's going on?"

"Miss Redwood, I'm surprised to see you here." I recognized the stern-faced Constable Cooper from that day at the bakery.

"I was picking up a book I lent Mr. MacNeil."

"Well, you'd best head home. Mr. MacNeil will be coming with us."

I slid past them to stand on Jack's lawn, casting a worried look at Jack.

"Don't worry, Bridget. It'll be okay."

I wasn't so sure as I watched the police lead Jack away.

Chapter 11: Revelations

Later that day, I ushered Hannah into the kitchen and blurted out the news. "The police took Jack. Wanted to question him about the murder."

"What? Why? This isn't what I expected when you called. After your text, I figured you two had deciphered the map."

"That got cut short by the police visit. He texted after to say he was okay, but I'm worried. I don't know the specifics, but I think the cops suspect he's involved in Johnson's murder."

"Is he?" Hannah dropped the question like a brick, staring straight at me. "Do you think they'll arrest him?"

I hesitated, wondering. Did I think Jack was involved? "He wasn't arrested, and, no, I don't think Jack's involved in the murder, not really. It's Jillian. I'm sure of it now. She came to the house fishing for information earlier." I sucked in a breath. "What if this is my fault?"

"Jack's troubles? How could that be your fault?"

"I told Jillian that the police didn't suspect me. What if she somehow set up Jack instead?"

"Now I'm confused. What's been going on here today?"

I filled Hannah in on Jack, Jillian's visit, and the map, showing her the book and what I already translated.

"Well, you've been busy." She fingered the edge of the map parchment. "So this thing is more written instructions than an actual map?"

"I guess. The whole thing is convoluted if you ask me."

Hannah shrugged. "Maybe Angus liked puzzles."

I laughed. The idea of a grizzled rumrunner having a fascination for puzzles struck me as funny. Poor Hannah looked aggrieved.

"Hey, it's possible. People have hobbies."

"Yeah, yeah, you're right. Sorry." I controlled my mirth. "We still have to figure out what to do. How do we help Jack?"

"We can't. He is either under suspicion of the murder or he isn't. That is out of our hands. And probably best we stay away from it for now. Do you want the police thinking you're Jack's accomplice? Or vice versa?"

I hadn't thought of that. "I guess you're right. I still feel awful leaving Jack out to dry."

"The best way to help him is finish what you both started." Hannah tapped the map. "We figure out what this means and find out what Angus was up to and why. We prove Jillian is responsible for the murder."

"You're right." I squared my shoulders. I might not have wanted this mess, but I was going to find a way out. For all of us.

"Good. I'll make some coffee and you get translating."

An hour and several cups of coffee later, we had jittery nerves and what we hoped was a finished translation of the map's text. Hannah gave her arms and back a stretch, echoed a minute later by Taffy, who then rubbed against my legs. I petted his ears and he started purring.

"Angus didn't make it easy, did he?" Hannah flopped back in her chair.

"No. Three different variants of the alphabet, and his poor handwriting. I hope we got it right."

"Read it back and we'll do a last proof check."

"After the midnight chime, go to Main Street by the statue.
To see the turn in time, recite the Chronos grimoire spell.
The map will show the crime, and you will know the truth."

I sighed. "Angus wasn't very poetic, was he?"

"No, but he was cryptic. We still don't know what spell he used to reveal whatever the heck he hid."

"Not exactly." I squirmed a bit. "I'm guessing his copy of the spell got lost somewhere over the years, but we still might find the original."

Hannah frowned. "The original?"

"It says the 'grimoire spell.' What grimoire do we know was connected to Angus?"

"Oh crap."

"Exactly. We're going to have to look in Marie's grimoire."

I brought the grimoire downstairs and laid it carefully on the kitchen counter, next to the candles, crystals, and runes Hannah set up. I slid the book out of the bag I wrapped it in; it still looked like an old research book.

"Is it dangerous to remove the disguise?" Hannah's voice quivered. "You said it's magic could be perceived when withdrawn."

I turned to her. "The wards on this house should prevent any detection, at least temporarily. We can't take too long, though. You ready?"

"Yeah, but not too happy about this." She sighed and wove the scrying spell, revealing the grimoire.

Magic infused the air and bounced off my skin. I reached out my hand, gently touching the worn leather cover, and a warm flush of power settled into my fingertips. A thrill raced up my spine as I sensed the essence of Marie's magic, as it connected to mine. The scents of magnolia and lemon wafted over me, with undertones of bourbon and smoky spice. An intoxicating electricity settled in my bones.

This is worth killing for.

I jerked my hand back at that thought and broke the connection.

Should we be doing this?

"Well? Are you going to open it?"

"Give me a second." Tentatively, I reached out again, but the effect of the magic was subdued this time, and I opened Marie LeBlanc's grimoire. The pages were crisp and slightly yellowed, not brittle with age as one might expect. As I carefully flipped through the book, the scent of jasmine floated in the air, with a hint of pine chasing it. A warm, comfortable feeling blended into my bones, as if I came home to a place I didn't know I'd been missing. I leafed through the pages and found the illustrated page with the spell mentioned on Angus' map.

I smiled. "I think this is it. The Chronos Revelation Spell. An enchantment to reveal a time imprint." I frowned. "Time imprint. Time imprint. I know that. Why does that— Oh my! Fire amber. I remember now." I rubbed my arm and swallowed, staring at Hannah. "Oh, this could be bad, and I may know why Angus wanted out. We have to see what's on this map and find that fire amber stat."

Hannah glanced at me, tilting her head. "How bad? What is it?"

"Marie may have been messing around with time travel. Fire amber was a thing back before cameras, used to record moments of time onto something like paper, or stone. Anything really. I think that's what Angus did with his map."

"That doesn't sound bad."

"It isn't. Fire amber only got banned in the 1800s when a witch, Rebecca Dobson, found it could also be used to manipulate time or even change the past. She created a spell to control it, but as far as I knew all copies were confiscated and destroyed. Hmmm, I wonder…" I turned back to the spell, taking a closer look. "Yeah, there's a notation from Marie about the Chronos spell's origin. It originated from Rebecca Dobson. And if Marie had one Dobson spell, maybe she had other, more dangerous spells. If fire amber is out there then we have to locate it."

"Oh." Hannah frowned, tapping a finger. "You're right, we need to figure this out. If this is what Jillian's after…" She shook her head. "We also have to warn the Council."

"Yeah. We do." I slumped over the grimoire. We'd have to turn everything over to them, including Marie's book. Something that left a hollow feeling in my gut. The lure of what was inside, all that magic…

"First, we find out what's on that map." Hannah's voice interrupted my musings. "You can do that, right?"

Surprised by the question, I replied, "Really? Why?"

"If we turn everything in now, we'll have to explain why we didn't turn over the grimoire and why we were messing with contraband. If we find the location of the fire amber, we can *fudge*," Hannah grinned at me as I glared, "some of the details about where and when we found the grimoire. They won't care how we cracked the map if we dangle two illicit prizes in front of them." Then she shrugged. "Besides, I'm curious. Before we get cut out, I want to know what happened between the conspirators. One last adventure before we act like responsible adults."

"Okay then." I hastily copied the spell, before reluctantly reactivating the grimoire's disguise. The temptation of its magic vanished, yet the memory of that taste lingered under my skin. With regret, I returned the grimoire to the hiding place.

When I came back downstairs, Hannah asked, "What now?"

I double-checked the spell and the translation. "The only ingredient we need is lavender oil, which I have. Angus' instructions clearly say after midnight to work the spell, so I guess we wait."

"We get to sneak around town in the wee hours? Hope we don't run into anyone coming home from the bar. It will be hard to explain what we're doing."

"Town square is usually deserted after midnight."

"How would you know that?"

"Don't ask." I grinned at her.

She rolled her eyes at me. "I guess we're watching Netflix for the rest of the day then."

Chapter 12: Back in Time

Shortly after midnight, dressed in stylish black, Hannah and I crept out of the house and snuck down to Main Street; our town square was the intersection at the far end. A soft warm glow bled from the street lamps, casting enough light, but the deserted, shadowy atmosphere made me nervous. We headed for the front lawn of the town hall, where the statue was erected, and stood in the chilly night air beside an effigy of a fisherman with his hands on a ship's wheel. We looked at each other.

"Now what?" Hannah stomped her feet and rubbed her arms to keep warm.

"Now we see what Angus imprinted on this so-called map." I dug it, the spell and a small vial of lavender oil out of my oversized purse. Then I stripped off my gloves, shoving them in a pocket.

"Hunker in close, I have to drop this oil around us in a circle." Hannah scooched in and we stood beside the statue facing the street; I made a circlet around us with the oil. "Okay, you hold the map and I'll recite the spell." I handed her the parchment and took a deep breath.

"Within the circle turn back time, beyond the sound of the midnight chime. Reveal events of the past, within the spell forever cast. Power of amber, power of fire, show us the moment we desire."

A glowing ring of magic rose above the circle of lavender oil, enveloping us inside, and Angus' map shimmered in a soft blue light. I felt dizzy and I grabbed Hannah's arm as her knees slightly buckled. In front of us modern Main Street dissolved in a pool of radiance and reformed into an old-fashioned roadway. From the clothes and the cars, it looked like the 1920s. And it was much earlier in the day, around late afternoon.

Hannah whispered, "Have we gone back in time?"

I shook my head, reaching out a finger to touch the translucent energy barrier that surrounded us. "No, we're observing an imprint, like a magical recording. But we are inside it. This is so weird."

"How do we get out?" Hannah's voice squeaked, her body trembled.

"Once the imprint plays out, the magic will fade away. Don't worry, we aren't trapped."

"Okay, I— Hey, there's one of the men from Marie's photo."

I turned my head, hearing the rattling sound of the traffic and the bleep of a car horn, and glimpsed a familiar looking man carrying a leather satchel hurrying down the road. We watched him dash along the street, collar turned up, hat pulled down, feet thumping against the ground, before the air shimmered and the scene changed.

"We're not on Main Street anymore." Hannah sounded intrigued. "We're down by the water. By the boat docks. Probably Harbour Drive. Or its 1920s equivalent." She sucked in a breath. "You can smell the salt air, and listen. Seagulls. The tide hitting the docks. This is amazing."

"Maybe not." My stomach churned.

"What? Why not?"

"That man, the satchel. I bet that was Angus. This might be the day he blew up the boat."

"Oh. I'm not sure I want to see *that*."

I nodded, but we didn't have any choice. The man we thought was Angus arrived, glancing around before sneaking onto a boat and going below deck. A few minutes later he scurried off the boat without his satchel, and hid in an alleyway across the street, his eyes fixed on the vessel he left.

Hannah gripped my arm. "Oh. Here comes Marie and George."

Helplessly, we stared as the laughing pair climbed onto the boat and motored out into the harbour, the chugging engine filling the silence like a countdown. Their boat sped towards the horizon as we held our breath, then met its fate in a fiery explosion that rang loud and awful in our ears. The docks erupted in a commotion as a few of the lingering fishermen scrambled to get their boats in the water for a rescue, racing to the flaming wreck. Shouts, engines, and crackling flames all melded in a cacophony of sound as we watched them fish something out of the water. When they returned, a moaning and injured George Johnson was brought ashore and the air shimmered once more.

As the vision began to fade, I glanced towards the alley; Angus was gone.

The horrible harbourside scene vanished, plunging us into a dark and murky in-between. I expected it to settle us back in the present, yet the time imprint wasn't done. We reemerged inside Marie's sanctuary, in the middle of an argument between Angus and Marie.

"You sorry excuse of a coward! You rat!" Marie spat at Angus, the spittle landing on his lapel. "Where is it, you thief?"

"Nowhere you'll find it, you bearcat!"

Marie hauled off and slapped Angus across the face with an audible *smack*. Hannah gasped, and for a minute I thought Angus might hit her back. The look on his face suggested he wanted to.

Marie snarled, "I ought to kill you. Or worse."

Angus smiled. "Then you'd never find it."

Marie smirked back. "You think you're so clever, nicking my fire amber. Hiding it. You've only set my plans back. I can get more. So why shouldn't I kill you?"

Angus laughed. "I ain't no fool. I kick it and the record of your plans goes straight to the Council. They'll come for you, if they know. If you think you can take on their bully boys, then rub me out. I dare you."

Marie flushed, her fingers twisting, curling into a fist.

"Get out," she hissed. "But watch your back, rat."

With her words, the vision faded, reforming back in the same room. Marie was gone and Angus was ransacking her desk.

What's he up to?

Then he laughed and plucked a glowing object out of a drawer. "Stupid woman. I knew you'd leave it here." Angus wrapped his prize in a dark cloth, stuffed it in his pocket, and headed to the door. He grunted and left the room.

I bet that was the fire amber.

Time shifted again in a swirl of light, transforming Marie's lair. We saw George, Angus and Marie sitting together drinking rum. I could feel the warm, stifling air and smell the sweat and alcohol.

Marie raised her glass. "To our success. May it only grow." She downed the rum in one shot, grinning like a madwoman.

"What is going on?" Hannah sounded annoyed. "This makes no sense."

"I think we're seeing everything in reverse. Angus must not have got the imprinting right. We're going backward through time."

Hannah rolled her eyes. "Great, we're stuck in a wonky time shift."

"Shh. We need to hear this."

We watched as Marie set down her empty shot glass with a laugh. "That's good hooch."

George sighed. "Are you going to let us in on the joke? You keep hinting at big plans, but telling us nothing. I'm beginning to think these schemes of yours are baloney."

"Poor George." Marie laughed again. "You know I like my games. I didn't have all the pieces until now. This arrived today." She patted a small parcel wrapped in brown paper and twine sitting on her desk. "Either of you two palookas know what fire amber is?"

George shook his head, but Angus hissed.

"Where did you get your hands on that stuff? It's dangerous."

Marie smiled. "Ain't nothing you can't get in this world if you know the right people. And sure, it's dangerous, yet you gotta take risks to get the reward."

Angus scowled, sipping on his rum.

George licked his lips. "What are you up to, doll?"

"Remember the spell broker we ran across in New York last trip out?"

Both George and Angus nodded.

"Well, I bought something special off him, something I didn't mention." She slipped a yellowed piece of paper from her pocket. "This here is a page from Rebecca Dobson's grimoire containing a very interesting spell. The Pendulum Spell. Wanna guess what it does?"

Angus stiffened, as George leaned forward eagerly, "Tell us, dollface."

"This little gem lets you manipulate time, boys. Open little pockets to view future events, travel to the past, even change things if you want. Think about it. Think about what we could do if we controlled time itself."

George let out a long whistle and then grinned. "We could control the world."

Angus said nothing. I saw his knuckles whiten as his hand tightened around his glass of rum.

"How does it work? What do we need?" George rubbed his hands together.

"Basic ingredients, mostly. And the fire amber. That's why I held off saying anything. It was a little touch-and-go there for a while. Didn't know if my guy would come through." Marie glanced at the package. "But he did. Want to see the stuff?"

George nodded and Marie unwrapped the package.

I leaned forward to get a better look. We needed to know how to recognize it.

Marie slid a long cylindrical shape from the brown paper. It resembled a wand, only much shorter, three inches in length, with carved grooves and etched runes. It earned its amber name, sparkling with a deep translucent golden colour. Yet at its heart pulsed a red glow, almost a burning fire, constantly shifting.

It's beautiful.

"That dinky thing is this fire amber?" George let the skepticism drip from his voice and then snorted. Marie scowled at him, but Angus answered.

"Don't let it fool you, that thing is powerful. Too powerful to be messed with." He slammed his shot glass down on a nearby table and stood. "You've gone over the edge, Marie, completely potty if you think you can use that spell of yours and not get caught. You'll bring the Council coppers down on us. I ain't getting rubbed out for some hair-brained scheme to control time."

"Do you think I'm that stupid?" Marie snapped. "The Council has to go first. No one is going to get in my way."

Angus stared. "You're planning on bumping off the Council? That's hokum."

Marie rose to her feet, her face flashing with anger. "No, It's sense. Aren't you tired of being controlled by a bunch of lily-livered, namby-pambies? All their rules and regulations, what has it ever gotten us? Not greenbacks. No, it's always the bum's rush for the likes of us. I want what I'm due and I'm going to take it." She sat back down and waggled the fire amber at Angus.

"You're screwy, Marie," Angus huffed, and walked out of the room.

The scene dissolved in a flash of light and we found ourselves back on Main Street a few seconds after the spell activated. As the magic dissolved, Hannah and I stepped out of the circle, staring at each other.

"Well, that was—"

"Where is the fire amber?"

We wheeled to see Jillian standing three feet from us brandishing a wand.

"Jillian!" I yanked my own wand from my purse and beside me I saw Hannah holding hers. "What are you doing here? Are you following us now?"

"Of course! How else am I going to know what you're up to, you sneak?"

"Sneak?" Hannah retorted, her tone annoyed. "Why are you out this late? Were you spying on us, or…" Hannah turned to me. "I bet she was trying to break into the bakery again and saw us."

Jillian shuffled her feet, her body language squirming. "Maybe I was at the bakery, but so what? You're up to no good, too." She moved closer, waving her wand. "Where is that fire amber? Tell me!"

I grimaced, ready for a fight. "No clue. You're wasting your time."

She scowled. "Don't mess with me! I saw you activate the map. You must know where Angus hid it."

"Sorry to disappoint, the map only showed Angus stealing it."

"Don't play me for a fool!" Jillian took another menacing step forward. "You activated the map! You need the amber to do that. Give it to me!"

I laughed. "You don't need fire amber to activate a time imprint, only to make one. Any competent witch who did her research would know that."

"You're lying!"

"No, but even if I had it, I wouldn't hand it over to you." Impulsively, I added, "I'm glad Marie's grimoire went down with her, in the boat, so you can't get your hands on it, either."

"What? You saw that?"

I nodded, enforcing the lie, and hoping Hannah would play along.

"Good. Then I don't have to worry about that counterspell. When I find the fire amber, no one will stop me."

"Wait? You already have the Pendulum Spell?"

"Oh, so you know about that too? Marie was smart. Sent a copy to her brother, who lived in Boston. And it turns out the LeBlancs and Burkes were related. I found the spell last year in an old trunk I inherited, along with an old letter detailing Angus' betrayal. I knew then what I needed to do. Tell me where the amber is, or I'll make you spill your secrets."

My shoulders tightened and I scowled at her. "I'd like to see you try. You up for a battle right here on Main Street, Jillian? You might be older than me, but I'm the better witch and we both know it."

"Plus, it's two against one," Hannah chimed in, moving to flank Jillian. "Do you think you can take on both of us?"

For a moment she hesitated, and then lowered her wand. "This isn't over, Redwood. Watch your back. You too, Murphy. And don't eat any fudge." She laughed and hurried away.

I nodded to Hannah, "Let's get out of here before she changes her mind."

"No way. We need to go after her. We can't let her escape."

"And do what? Fight her? In the middle of town? We'd get arrested for assault or worse. We've no proof to show the police."

"So, she goes on her merry way, until she finds what she needs and does who knows what?"

"No. We may not have proof for the police, but I think we have enough for the Council. We need to wake up some people."

Chapter 13: The Council

After several knocks and angry encounters with sleepy people, we had a Council meeting ready to convene. As the elder witches arrived at the community centre, my nerves jangled and my throat felt dry.

Would we be able to convince them? How much do we tell them?

Part of me wanted to come clean with everything we found, wash my hands of the whole mess, but I couldn't shake the desire to keep the grimoire.

What if we needed it again?

I stared at the Council as they took their seats.

Can we trust them?

On impulse, I leaned over and whispered to Hannah, "Please, follow my lead."

With a sideways glance, she asked, "Why? What are you up to?"

"Trust me."

"I guess…" She didn't sound convinced.

One of the men beckoned us forward and we shuffled to the table where they were seated. Hannah grabbed my hand

and I felt her trembling as we faced four sleepy, annoyed Council members.

Mr. Landry stared at us. "This better be good."

I took a deep breath. "It is, sir. There is a rogue witch running around Easthaven Bay looking for a hidden stash of fire amber."

That got their attention, and they hung on our every word as I detailed the encounters with Johnson's ghost, finding the hidden room and Marie's journal, the revelations of the time imprint and being confronted by Jillian. I left out the part about locating the grimoire and using it to decipher the map.

"Well, you two have been busy." An older woman, Anne Forbes, gave us a disapproving look. "Why didn't you come to us sooner?"

Hannah ducked her head and stared at her feet. I squeezed her hand.

"Hannah wanted to, but I wasn't sure who to trust at first, who might be involved. And I thought it best to wait until we had more solid proof of a crime. I didn't want to make any false accusations. Until tonight, we only had speculation and theory."

Anne Forbes frowned. "I suppose I can understand that, though it was reckless of you." I nodded and did my best to look chastised as she continued, "Is there any indication she was working with someone?"

"As far as we know, only Mr. Johnson, the poor man."

"Well, that's a blessing. A full investigation of the coven is never a pleasant undertaking. Bad enough we'll have to deal with Ms. Burke. You can leave this matter in our hands now. No more amateur sleuthing. Or we may have to deal with you both as well." She glared, an icy look that definitely meant business.

"Yes, ma'am. Fine by me." I exhaled softly and glanced at Hannah when I felt her let go of my hand.

Her rigid posture and crossed arms told me she was upset and she met my gaze with disappointment before looking back to the Council. I thought she might say something, yet she remained silent about my omissions.

I'd deal with her feelings later. There was one more thing I needed to know.

"What about the murder? We have no real proof Jillian's responsible, and I still have a restless spirit haunting my house. Not to mention, Jack MacNeil is under suspicion for the crime."

"Yes, we heard the police questioned Jack. They didn't arrest him, though. We'll deal with the murder as well, don't worry."

I nodded, ushering Hannah out of the building as she glared at me. She didn't say one word during the walk back to my house, but I knew what she was thinking.

"Why didn't you tell them about the grimoire?" Hannah barked at me the minute we were inside the house. "We agreed."

"I know, I know. I'm sorry, but, well, I thought about it and decided it's not the right time."

"Not the right time? What kind of lame excuse is that?"

"The only one I have." I snapped, getting defensive. "And if you are so worried, why didn't you tell the Council? Huh, why?"

"Because I'm your friend, and I'm not going to sell you out. Ride or die, remember? I don't want either of us in trouble."

"Oh." Guilt rushed in, crushing my annoyance. "Thanks for not ratting on me. I know you're anxious; so am I. It's a risk keeping the grimoire, but we don't know who we can trust. Is Jillian working alone?"

I took a breath, stuffing my guilt past my need to convince her. "What if we turn it over and someone steals it? As long as it's hidden, everyone is safe. I think it's better we wait, to see how things unfold before we let the Council have it." Perfectly plausible excuses. "Besides, how would we explain why we had it? That we didn't turn it over right away? We need to craft a credible story."

Hannah frowned. "And no other reason?" She stared, coming dangerously close to her *'don't lie to me'* look.

I tried not to squirm. "I don't know what you mean?" Hannah didn't need to know about the pull of Marie's magic.

"It feels like there's something you're not telling me."

"Well…" For a minute I wanted to tell her the truth, but didn't, only adding, "We could use some leverage. Maybe find that counterspell Jillian mentioned, or another safeguard. In case the Council can't stop her."

"You are making sense, I guess. I'm still not comfortable with this. It seems chancy. You will turn it over eventually, right?"

Would I though? Maybe.

I smiled at Hannah. "As soon as Jillian's been dealt with, I'll tell the Council, come up with an excuse about finding it. I'll even keep you out of it."

"Okay. I guess I can go along with that. As long as you know I'm here if you need me. We are in this together, Bridget."

I nodded, happy she capitulated.

Hannah let out an exaggerated sigh. "How did things get so complicated so quickly? Everything we find leads to a bigger mystery." She rubbed the back of her neck. "I'm so wired. I know it's late, but I can't sleep yet."

Willing to steer the conversation in a different direction, I asked, "How about some ice cream?"

"Oh, that sounds good."

"I'm glad the Council's involved, but I'll miss the investigation." Hannah drowned her sorrows in an overflowing spoonful of chocolate mint ice cream.

"What's left to investigate? We found the secret room, we know what happened between Angus, George and Marie, and Jillian all but confessed to the murder."

"She didn't, though. Confess. Sure, she's the one behind Johnson breaking into your place, and she's up to no good, yet what proof is there that she killed him?"

"What? Where did this come from?"

"I don't know. I feel like we're missing something. Jillian's guilt is based on our assumptions, not proof. Here." She rummaged in her purse and pulled out a notebook and pen. "I put all the facts down in a list." She cleared her throat and squared back her shoulders.

"Fact one: There are three items people wanted. Marie's grimoire, Angus' map, and the fire amber. Fact two: They were all connected. The grimoire held the spells, or people suspected it did, the amber was the key to the spells and everyone thought Angus' map showed the location of the amber."

I nodded, thinking. "Which it didn't. Jillian thought it did, and so did the MacNeils and the Johnsons. I wonder why?"

Hannah frowned. "That is strange, but we can worry about that later. Fact three: We don't know Jillian had a motive for murder."

"What? Of course we do. She was behind the shop break-ins, remember. She found out about Johnson's double-cross, or he was blackmailing her."

"Johnson might have been blackmailing a lot of people, are we suspecting them too? As for who he double-crossed, we brought Jillian's name into it, not Johnson."

"Didn't he?" I frowned, thinking back. His ramblings were incoherent. Maybe we did make assumptions. "Okay, but they were partners. And he was greedy. It could be a motive."

"Possibly," Hannah nodded. "I think that's what's bothering me. Why kill him? If it was blackmail, Jillian could have paid him off. Or threatened him back. After all, he was committing crimes for her and dealing in black market magical items. She had dirt on him, too. Plus, why was he in the bakery that night? Why was he still looking for the grimoire? Jillian didn't even want it that badly. Not if her reaction to your lie was any indication. She wanted the fire amber."

"Now that is a good point. Was he still working for Jillian that night, or for himself? Did he actually locate Marie's room or stumble across the discrepancy in the blueprints?"

Hannah tapped her notepad, and then scribbled with her pen. "That's a good possibility."

"What else is in your notes?"

"You may not like this one. Fact four: The police questioned Jack. Why? A brief argument in your bakery is pretty thin to bring someone into the police station for formal questioning. There must be something more to their relationship."

I scowled at Hannah; her reasoning made me uneasy. "Jack explained that. Johnson was after the map. The police probably found that out."

"Which leads to fact five: Jack had a possible motive. Johnson wanted Angus' map. Was Jack angry about that?"

"That seems like a thin motive." Then something occurred to me. "Do you know which of the MacNeils owned the map?"

Hannah flipped through her notes. "I did check that out. The only info I dug up was that Jack's grandfather owned it. Who inherited it after his death, I don't know."

"Jack did." The words tumbled out. "He has a trunk with his grandfather's things. That's where I got the book on the Theban alphabet."

"That could explain the animosity. If Johnson was pestering Jack to sell the map, things could have gotten heated."

"Enough animosity to lead to murder?" I shook my head. "I don't know if I buy it. Besides, can you see Jack obtaining cyanide without it being traced? He's not a criminal mastermind or a chemistry whiz."

Hannah frowned. "You got me there, although he might have found enough info on the internet."

"True, but that logic applies to Jillian as well. Plus, she has the money to have bought the poison on the black market."

"I guess." Hannah put down her notes. "Jillian is a good suspect. I still feel like we're missing something."

"Well, it's too late to figure it out tonight." I scooped up the empty ice cream dishes and dumped them in the sink. "Let's get some sleep. You can crash in the guest room, if you want."

"Thanks. I don't feel like trekking home this late."

I locked up, turned out the lights and we headed upstairs to crash.

I hope things settle down now.

Chapter 14: Sweet Temptation

After a late breakfast the next morning, Hannah and I parted ways, and for the first time since the murder I didn't feel stressed. I lounged in my pajamas until lunch, ate a leisurely meal, before I took a long relaxing bath.

Lighting some candles, I filled the tub with jasmine-scented foaming bubble bath, and on a whim, I found a 1920s jazz playlist on my phone. As the sweet music filled the room, I slipped into the tub, letting the heat soak into my skin. I inhaled the floral aroma swirling in the water as it mixed with the fragrance of the lavender-scented candles.

This is the life.

Until my phone buzzed with the sound of an incoming text.

I ignored it. Then it buzzed again. And again.

I sighed and got out of the tub. After drying off and putting on clean pajamas and a bathrobe, I checked my messages. All the texts were from Hannah.

The Council talked to Jillian. She denied everything. Tried to blame us.

The Council is back in meetings!!!

Are you there??
What if they decide to investigate what we've been up to?
We could be in trouble!!!!!

Why aren't you replying!!!!!

I texted back.
Don't panic.
Of course, she denied it and blamed us.
But the Council is smart.

Another buzz. Hannah sent another text.
What if they know what you're hiding?
We shouldn't have kept it.

Annoyed, I replied,
If they knew, they'd be knocking on our doors.
Don't worry.
We are the only people who know.

Another reply from Hannah.
You'd better be right. And she added a worried face emoji.

I left the conversation there, and turned the phone off, heading across the hall to my bedroom. I flopped on the bed and glared at my closet.

"This is all your fault, Marie. You and that grimoire of yours. I should have turned it over. Now I have Hannah mad at me."

Why didn't I turn it over?

Curiosity, to spite my mother, desire for magic? And why did I feel such a connection when I first touched it? What did Marie do to it? It had been ages since I craved the study of powerful magic.

Maybe I should investigate and find out.

I wanted to. The desire to run my fingers over the leather and feel the texture of pages and smell the ink was strong. I slid my legs over the edge of the bed, staring at the closet. A draft of air wafted the smell of jasmine in the room.

Do it. You need to know.

I walked to the closet and opened the door, and the next thing I knew the book was sitting on top of my bedspread. I laid a hand on top, humming a bit of old-fashioned jazz, hoping to feel the power, but Marie's disguise was too strong. To get what I craved, I needed to reveal the grimoire.

It'll be alright, just this once.

I took a breath trying to convince myself, looking for excuses.

I'll look for the counterspell Jillian mentioned. We might need it.

I scrambled off the bed again and raced downstairs for the supplies, hauling the candles, crystals and runes back to the bedroom and activated the spell. And there it was, the beautiful leather-bound book with its siren's call of magic. I figured I had an hour with it, before the grimoire's energy penetrated my wards, potentially alerting people to its presence. So, I set an alarm, snuggled under the covers and started flipping pages.

The same scent of magnolia and lemon drifted into the air, and this time a warmth infused my fingers, settling across my skin like a familiar cozy blanket. The book didn't feel strange and intimidating anymore; it felt like mine.

All mine.

I skimmed the spells, reading the names. Some were standard spells, some variations on things I knew. Others were dark conjurations with names such as Darkness of Breath, Curse of the Undead, Malediction of the Void. I lingered with those, reading and studying how they worked and the ingredients needed. Each time I did, I felt closer to the grimoire, more connected, experiencing heady scents of jasmine, smoke, and rose with frissons of energy racing against my fingertips.

I barely watched the clock, not caring anymore whether anyone knew I had the grimoire. No one was going to take it away from me. Not with this magic in my control. Marie was a genius, and her spellwork was unlike anything I had seen before. No restrictions, no rules, only the purity of being a witch.

Oh, what I could do with this. Mother would never tell me what to do again.

I turned another page and a folded letter fell into my lap as the alarm blared in my ear. The combination startled me and I closed the book with a snap, breaking the captivation I was under. Chilled, I shoved the grimoire away from me and a breath of air caused by the movement blew out one of the candles. Immediately, the grimoire disappeared into its disguise and I snapped back to myself.

What just happened?

I stared at the book for a minute before stuffing it back in its bag and shoving it out of sight in the closet. I extinguished the rest of the candles and returned all the ingredients back downstairs. Coming back to the bedroom, I noticed the letter was still on the bed.

Gingerly picking it up with two fingers, it radiated nothing magical, so I unfolded it. Written in Marie's handwriting, it was a letter to her mother. Curious, I settled in to read it.

Dear Mama,

I do not know whether I will have the courage to send this or not, but for my own peace of mind I must write this letter. I cannot live with the burden of your scorn, of your restrictions. I will no longer live within the small narrow world you wish to force upon me, the life of the dutiful daughter, heir to the grand witch Madeleine LeBlanc.

A shiver arced across my skin. Marie's words echoed my own thoughts and feelings regarding my mother. How much do we have in common, her and I? Is that why I felt so connected to her grimoire?

I know you were the one who betrayed Andre, because I dared defy you, because I dared love someone you deemed unworthy. It is too late, Mama; he has opened my eyes. He may be gone, six feet under the ground, yet I will not bow to anyone again, least of all you. I won't repress the nature of my magic or conform to your foolish rules, when true power is mine for the taking.

What do I care about right and wrong? You don't.

You had a man killed, not to protect me as you claim, but to control me. Bring me in line with your politics, your rigid society of witches. I renounce you and your coven. I renounce all covens. From this day, I vow to devote myself to the study and pursuit of magic, all magic, no matter whether it is accepted practice or not. I will make my position in this world the way I see fit.

I will not be you.

I will not force myself to be molded in the ways of others.

You may think me misguided and foolish, you may disown me, but I will be a better person than you, Mama.

Your daughter, (for now) Marie
July, 13, 1912

I laid the letter down and stared at it. So, Marie had issues with her mother too? And she had more courage than I did. She didn't send the letter, yet she made the clean break.

It all went wrong, though.

What happened, Marie? Did your pursuit of magic corrupt your ethics? You wanted to be better than your mother. Like me. Yet you failed. I glanced at the closet.

Am I failing too?

I folded the letter and slid it in my nightstand drawer. I had a lot to think about.

The next morning, I stood in front of the closet, trying to summon the courage to handle the grimoire. After reading the letter and a restless night, I decided to turn over the book to the Council. Yet, here I was, not moving.

Open the door.

With a deep breath, I turned the knob and yanked open the closet. It sat, waiting on the top shelf. I couldn't make myself reach up.

How are you going to explain why you have the book?

Maybe I shouldn't do this? No, I only need a plausible excuse. Maybe push the timeline up. Say I thought of the disguise angle recently, and not when we found the room. That would work, I guess.

Then pick it up and bring it with you.

I closed the closet door.

No, better let them come and get it. I'll call them.

I went downstairs and made some coffee and breakfast, putting off dealing with the grimoire until a knock sounded on the door. I jumped, spooked, before taking a breath.

Calm down and answer it. It isn't the Council.

Hannah waited on my doorstep, an annoyed look on her face. She didn't say hello, only pushed past me into the hall. I shut the door to preserve our privacy.

She faced me, arms crossed, and blurted, "Talk to me. What's going on with you? Why do you really want to keep the grimoire?"

"I told you. I'm concerned Jillian could find out. And then how long before she found a way to steal it?"

"Yeah, except Jillian's not interested in the grimoire. In fact, you're the only one interested in that book. Why?"

Irritation welled, and I curled my fingers, anger edging under my skin. "Because we need to protect it!"

"Protect it from what? Who is the threat?"

How could she understand? The book was mine.

I glared and ignored the question.

Hannah sighed. "This has to end. And as much as I care, I should have never agreed to let you keep it. You have to give the grimoire to the Council."

Who was she to tell me what to do?

I took a breath and plastered a fake smile on my face.

"It's safer here. For now." I tried to sound convincing, maybe more for myself, than Hannah.

Hannah shook her head. "No, it's not. If that book is discovered, Jillian could use it against you." She laid a hand on my arm. "I don't like this game you're playing. Promise me you'll turn it over soon."

I clenched my jaw.

I'll tell her what she wants to hear.

I replied, "Okay, I promise. Soon. Give me until after the bakery reopens."

Hannah nodded, stalking out of the house without another word. I wasn't certain she believed me and I didn't care.

Chapter 15: Exploration

The next day didn't go well, as I avoided Hannah's texts, as well as messages from Jack, and hid out in my house, away from everyone; the only contact I had was with my employees and the cleaning crew to make sure things were going smoothly for the reopening. The complications in my life kept compounding, and all day my mind wandered to the grimoire hidden upstairs. I resisted until after supper, then I brought the book downstairs to the living room. I had arranged the runes, crystals, and candles on the coffee table, so I placed the grimoire beside them. I only needed to light the candles to begin.

Should I?

I reached for the matches, despite my reservations.

Just a peek. I still need to find that counterspell Jillian mentioned.

Lighting a match, I hovered my hand over the first candle.

If I get it out of my system, it will be easier to turn the book over.

I lit the candles and inhaled the scent of magnolias and lemon as the familiar leather cover revealed itself. A shiver of glee raced across my skin and I hit the fifty-minute timer on my phone.

Snuggling under a blanket on the couch, I took a leisurely approach to studying the grimoire, starting from the beginning and reading each spell, examining Marie's work, savouring the texture of the paper under my fingertips. The book's smoky warm energy seeped into my pores, filling me with an intoxication, like drinking fine bourbon. Nothing beyond reading the grimoire mattered anymore; Marie's magic meant everything.

When the alarm blared, disappointment surged, but I blew out the candles because I had a plan. I checked my wards to see if they were still in place, and nothing seemed amiss. Then I reset the alarms, waited a few minutes before relighting the candles and settled in for another fifty-minute reading session.

I smiled as I sank back into the comforting feeling of the grimoire; the further I read, the more it felt like it belonged to me. I absorbed the words and spells with a profound sense of potency and joy. When the second round of the timer went off, I eagerly dived back in for round three.

It was during this session I finally stumbled on the counterspell and hastily scribbled it down on a scrap of paper as I read.

Unwinding Spell
(How to Reverse the Pendulum Spell)

What you need: One pendulum

Incantation:
As the pendulum swings, rewind the thread
that clock unwound, what time unbound
undo the breaks and stitch them back
reverse the harm and seal the cracks
As the pendulum swings, rewind the thread

Swing the pendulum in a counterclockwise circle and recite the incantation three times. Then swing the pendulum in a clockwise direction and recite the incantation three times. This will reverse any alterations in time created while using the Pendulum Spell with the Fire Amber.

I noticed beneath the spell Marie wrote some additional notes.

Rebecca was a chump. Her use of the Pendulum Spell got her in a jam with a time paradox, her alterations rendering her sorcery bunk and initiated endless temporal loops. Seems she tried to influence her own life, her own actions, and got behind the eight ball. Have to avoid changing my personal circumstances. Any individual cause and effect will conjure a loop of the new timeline, ever collapsing in on itself and perpetually resetting. In case things go sideways, this incantation safeguards against blunders and won't leave me holding the bag. Any changes can be undone when the need arises. With this I'll be the cat's meow.

As I read the last line, the timer went off and I blew out the candles. Glancing at the clock, I realized it was close to 10 PM. I had the bakery reopening tomorrow. I should stop, put the book away. I found what I was looking for.

Yet there's so much more to find.

I closed my eyes and hugged the book. *I don't want to give this to the Council. Why is Hannah making me do that? I thought we were friends.*

I could make her forget. There was a spell for that in the grimoire.

Yeah, I could make her think the grimoire went down with the boat. Then nobody would know but me. And it would be my grimoire. Forever. I smiled and stroked the book. I liked the plan and I could take my time, study and learn all of Marie's secrets. Then they would be mine. If I used the grimoire to strengthen my wards, I could remove the disguise permanently, access it anytime I wanted.

Satisfied, I cleaned up and got ready for bed, tucking the grimoire back into its hiding place. Then I snuggled under the covers, drifting off to sleep…

I heard music, the soft subtle notes of a jazz piano. Warm light infused the…where am I? Is this a room?

"You're in the world between, chère. The world of dreaming."

A familiar voice drifted out of the ether. Silky and feminine with a New Orleans accent. "Marie LeBlanc?"

"Of course." A woman materialized in front of me, bobbed dark hair, dark eyes, wearing a silky beaded flapper dress and a long fur coat. She looked like she stepped out of a 1920s speakeasy. A whiff of her jasmine perfume tickled my nose.

"I'm dreaming?" It had to be; I didn't want anymore ghosts in my life.

"A dream, a memory, a desire? Maybe it's all the same, chère. Whatever the reason, you got a taste, like that first sip of hooch, and you want more. So, you came to see me."

"A taste of what?"

"The magic. It seeps into your bones. That appetite for power, throwing away the rules. You and I, we're dames of a feather. We're better than those rubes and saps. We take what we want, and don't let nobody stand in our way. Like that friend of yours, Hannah."

"She's not in my way."

"She's standing between you and keeping my grimoire, ain't she? You didn't hesitate in making a plan. Shows promise." Marie sashayed over to me and stroked my cheek.

Her touch was like fire and I breathed in her scent, my senses heady with jasmine and a hint of bourbon. "What do you want from me?"

"I like you. You could be somebody. I could show you how." She twirled a lock of my hair around her finger and laughed. "I know you want it."

"What do I want?"

"Take a look in the mirror."

I turned and saw my reflection in a full-length mirror, standing there in pajamas. Then Marie slipped her fur coat over my shoulders. The mirror shimmered and my reflection transformed; underneath Marie's coat I wore a beautiful lacy green dress, my red hair now styled in a short bob with a cloche hat perched on top.

"You look spiffy in those rags, chère." Marie's voice whispered in my ear, "Really beautiful, powerful. A looker." She caressed my arm and I shivered. "What you and I could have done, back in the day. Maybe we still could."

"What are you talking about? This is a dream."

"Is it? Or is it what you desire, chère?" Her fingers stroked my hip. "You like the allure of the darker magicks, I can feel that. We have that in common, you and I. Together we could rule this world. One spirit, one heart. All you have to do is let me in."

Marie spun me around, her face inches from mine, her arms slipping around my waist. The fur coat fell in a mess around my feet as she pulled me close and I slid my arms around her neck. I closed my eyes as her lips touched mine and we kissed, long and deep. Her essence, her spirit, her magic melded into me, infusing my body with an exhilarating power. When I opened my eyes, she was gone; I could still feel the taste of her in my mouth, under my skin, the itch of her thoughts in my head.

"What did you do to me?"

"Look." Her voice echoed in my mind.

I turned back to the mirror, and Marie's face stared back from my reflection.

I screamed as the echo of Marie's laughter surrounded me.

I sat upright in bed, fully awake, and then scrambled to my feet racing to the bathroom. My own face stared at me from the mirror. I sighed in relief. The feeling of dark power and Marie's spirit had disappeared too.

A dream. Just a dream.

Stumbling back to bed, I glanced at the closet and shivered.

No. No more. I won't become Marie. It goes to the Council tomorrow.

Chapter 16: Ghostly Investigation

The next morning, still shaken, I rose with the dawn and headed to the bakery. Despite everything, I had a reopening today, and eager employees ready to get back to work; I'd deal with the grimoire afterward. It would be a shorter work day for the shop, and we spent the morning baking, ready for business in time for lunch. I tried to forget the dream, but my thoughts strayed back to the nightmare.

Don't think about that, concentrate on business.

I anticipated a slow day, as I hadn't done any advance advertising about reopening, yet business was brisk from the moment I opened the doors. I should have expected the town gossip mill would spread the word that the bakery was serving again.

Of course, everyone was talking about the murder, offering their sympathies to me, and a few pressed me for lurid details about finding the body. I smiled through the lunch crowd, offering as little information as possible, but by late afternoon I planned to call it quits, leave the front counter to one of my assistants and hide in the back with the baking.

Until Esther walked in the shop and dropped a bombshell as she ordered her chocolate walnut brownies. She leaned in and asked, "Have you heard about Jillian? She's gone missing."

I froze, my mind in a sudden panic. Trying to keep the trembling out of my voice I asked, "Missing? What do you mean missing?"

"She hasn't been seen since the day before yesterday, not since she had supper at the Wanderers Grill." Then she whispered, "I heard the coven Council sent folks out to her place to have a chat and now she's done a runner. I hear the police are looking for her too, regarding the murder."

A shiver ran across my skin. Jillian was on the run from the Council and the police? What was she up to now? Would she come back here looking for the fire amber again? I hoped not.

"Who would have thought Jillian would be a suspect? I guess the police are keen on her for some reason." Esther continued to blather as I packed her brownies. "Never struck me as someone willing to get her hands dirty by killing someone, but they do say poison is a woman's weapon. Guess you never know people, do you?" Esther waved goodbye and she and her brownies exited the shop.

I flagged my employee, Johnnie. "Take over the counter, will you?" I asked and fled to the back, my hands shaking.

What if Jillian comes after me again?

That thought gave me a shiver.

Maybe I should hang on to the grimoire for protection? No, stop thinking like that. That thing is trouble. I wish I never heard of Marie LeBlanc or her stupid schemes.

I gave my bakery ceiling a glare. How did I get so messed up in this?

I knew investigating was going to be trouble.

The rest of the day unfolded with more of the same, the curious popping in for gossip and pastries, and Jillian became the hot topic as the day wore on. I stayed away from the front as much as possible, although I eavesdropped on snippets of conversation, trying to find out if anyone knew anything.

"Can't say I ever liked the woman. Too stuck up for her own good. Not surprised she turned out to be a bad egg."

"One of those rich snobs. Thinking she can do whatever she wants."

"She never fit in here. Not surprised she's involved somehow."

"Always trying to give her opinion. Too uppity. She's getting what's coming to her. You'll see."

Every opinion seemed to be against Jillian, and no one seemed to offer facts as to why she would kill Johnson. Every voice I heard an echo of my own bias against her, the way she reminded me of my mother and her friends, how her superior attitude annoyed me. Doubts of her guilt seeped in as I realized my own quick judgement. Did my dislike of the woman unfairly single her out for me as a suspect?

What if I got it wrong?

Maybe Hannah was right to doubt, yet Jillian was involved somehow. The question that kept nagging at me was, how much? Jillian was a rogue witch, no doubt, and not a nice person. Was she a murderer, though?

As much as I wanted it wrapped up and done, I wasn't so sure anymore. We might be missing something.

When I arrived home after closing the bakery, I called the coven secretary and made an appointment the next day to convene the Council. Better to turn the grimoire over in person and spin some lies to keep myself out of trouble.

After that, all I wanted was food and a glass of wine. Maybe a mindless movie or a good book to soothe my emotions. Yet, I flopped on the couch, my mind muddled with trying to sort out my conflicting thoughts.

Why am I obsessing anyway? It's none of my business. Let the Council handle it.

The cold lump in my stomach said otherwise, though. I was part of this whether I liked it or not. I had poked my nose in too far.

How do I get answers?

"Why did Johnson have to get murdered in my bakery?" I shouted my frustration and sat up, staring blankly at the wall for a minute before it hit me. There was one person I could talk to for answers, but I'd have to ask the right questions.

I'd have to summon the ghost of Jeffery Johnson again.

I slumped on my couch with a sigh.

After a good meal and maybe one too many glasses of wine, I was feeling more composed and still sober enough to work the summoning spell. Soon enough a familiar apparition materialized in my living room.

The ghost hovered there with a confused look on his face. I knew the feeling.

"You and I need to have a chat, Mr. Johnson, and this time I want answers."

The ghost moaned.

"Oh, stuff it, this should be easy for you to answer." I took a deep breath, and consulted the notes I made, hoping I phrased things right. If I asked no questions about his death, maybe I could circumvent whatever block prevented him from talking. I had considered showing him a list of suspect names, but any decent spell would prevent him from pointing out the guilty party.

Facing the ghost, I asked, "Why were you at the bakery that night? Did someone send you?"

He shook his head. "After grimoire... for me. Double-cross."

"Okay, so you were double-crossing whoever you were working for? Planning on stealing the grimoire for yourself?"

The ghost nodded.

"Why?"

"Money. Big black market money..."

"I'll bet. Probably would've been a bidding war to get it."

The ghost moaned again. Whether from pain or the loss of the cash, I didn't know.

I glanced down at my list. "Was anyone with you that night? Did you see anyone in the bakery?"

Another shake of its head.

"Were you working for anyone besides Jillian?"

Johnson's ghost nodded, his head bobbing up and down like a fishing lure. A chill chased down my spine.

Why didn't we think to do this earlier? Wasting time trying to get names instead of facts. I sighed. *Because I wanted to take shortcuts.*

Well not anymore. Next question. "Was this other person after the fire amber or the map?"

"No… only Jillian."

"Jillian was the only one who was interested in those things?"

"Yes."

"Was this other person after the grimoire?"

The ghost nodded, its form wavering. Okay, that one hit a little too close. Funny though, Jillian's name didn't trigger anything.

I took a breath. I decided to take a chance. I hoped diverting from my list didn't break the connection. "Was Jillian after the grimoire?"

"Not really… More interested in map."

"Yeah, she would be. She thought it led to the fire amber."

"Yes, yes…" The ghost's form waggled excitedly.

"Well, it didn't. Sorry." Another moan. "Was Jillian working with anyone besides you?"

"No…too greedy. Didn't even pay me…"

"Offered you a cut?" He nodded. "And you—you took it? Oh, wait, you were planning on that double cross all along." I glared at the ghost. Then something occurred to me.

"Jillian wasn't the only one you double crossed. If this other person wanted the grimoire, you planned to screw them over too."

The ghost wavered, fading out before rematerializing.

"I'm right! That gave them a motive. Were they the one that killed you? Tell me. Try and give me a name!"

Johnson's apparition dissolved in and of reality, screaming, but somehow managed to choke out the words, "Yes, other… it was…" before snapping from the plane of reality and disappearing.

"Well, drat. Jillian wasn't responsible for the murder."

I collapsed down on the couch trying to absorb the news.

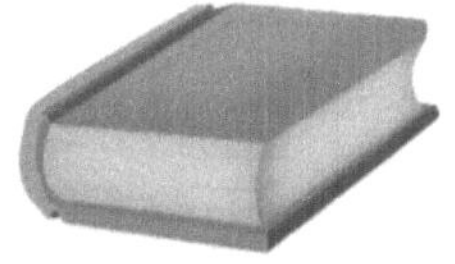

Chapter 17: Guilty!

I had to throw out everything I thought I knew and start over. This wasn't about the fire amber, or the map, it was about Marie's grimoire. I knew how Jillian found out about the grimoire; family connections to Marie. How did the real killer know?

Hannah said it was part of the town witch lore, so anyone in the coven could know. Could Emily or Sarah have figured things out from hanging out with Jillian? Maybe.

The Johnsons had known, but Jeffery was the last Johnson in town as far as I knew. That left the MacNeils. Any one of them could have made a play for the grimoire, especially with Johnson sniffing around about Angus' map.

Even Jack.

Would Jack have hired Johnson? I found that hard to believe. Even before this mess, Jack didn't think highly of my former landlord. He certainly didn't trust him. Why would he hire him to find Marie's book?

Still, it made the most sense that Jack would be the MacNeil involved. He knew Johnson wanted to buy the map, and he had to have suspected Johnson was after Marie's secrets.

Why hire Johnson to find the grimoire? Why not go after it himself? That's the part that didn't make any sense to me.

So how to prove one way or the other if Jack was the other partner?

I had no conventional proof to take to the police or the Council; neither one would take the word of an unreliable ghost that had been a cheat and a liar in life. So how to conjure up some magical insight? Some kind of spell to confirm or deny Jack's guilt? I frowned, thinking.

A truth spell maybe? Bake him a treat with a little surprise inside.

The thought of that made me queasy. I never liked messing with people, even if my ethics had been a bit shaky of late. Love potions, truth spells, any kind of manipulation didn't sit well with me. These weren't ordinary circumstances, though, and I might have to bend my morals a bit more. With a sigh, I went and fetched one of my spellbooks.

Flipping through the pages, I found something that might work without compromising my conscience or crossing any lines. A magical lie detector of sorts. The spell would make any object glow in the presence of a lie. I smiled.

My very own witchy polygraph test. Perfect.

Now what to use for the object? Something that wouldn't look suspicious for me to carry around or…wear.

Yeah, that would work.

I raced upstairs and rooted through my jewelry box until I found a cute teardrop pendant and bounded back down to cast the spell.

Gathering the ingredients, I laid the necklace on the table and placed a purple candle beside it. I trickled a drop of peppermint oil on the gemstone teardrop and then poured a circle of ginger root powder around the piece of jewelry. Then I lit the candle and recited the spell.

"Unwrap the lies,
that fall from lips,
in truth's bright glow
for deceit's eclipse."

The candle flame glowed a bright, pale violet and the teardrop gem shone in a matching radiance, while the room infused with the mingling scents of ginger and peppermint. Magic raced around the circle of spice before embedding itself into the pendant. The candle flame died and it was done. I picked up my necklace, wiping off the excess oil, and fastened it around my neck. Then I cleaned up the remaining ginger, put away the candle and my spellbook, before making myself a cup of chamomile tea.

I was sitting on the couch relaxing, wondering whether I should make a late evening visit to Jack or wait until morning when a knock on the door interrupted my thoughts. I put the tea down with some annoyance and answered the door. Jack was standing there.

"Sorry to pop in this late, but I needed to see you." He stepped inside without an invitation and I closed the door behind us with some trepidation. I wasn't expecting this. I fingered the chain of my necklace.

Can I do this?

I brushed past him asking, "Do you want some tea? Or maybe coffee?"

"Um, yeah. Coffee would be nice. Instant's fine. No need to make a pot."

I nodded, retrieved my tea and we headed to the kitchen. I made the coffee, handed Jack the cup, took a deep breath and asked, "Why did you need to see me tonight?"

"I, um," He ducked his head and stared into his coffee. "I heard about Jillian and I wanted to check on you. I was worried." He lifted his head and grinned. That stupid boyish smile made my heart beat faster.

Don't let his good looks distract you.

"That was sweet of you, but she's probably long gone from Easthaven Bay."

"Maybe, yet she didn't get what she wanted, did she?"

"No." I sipped my tea, taking comfort in the warmth. "What she was looking for is lost."

"Marie's grimoire, you mean?"

So, you knew about that, did you?

"No, not really. I think Johnson was searching my bakery after hours, trying to find Marie's sanctuary and fire amber. Jillian wasn't after the grimoire." I finished my tea and turned back to put the cup in the sink before I told my lie. "I think

the grimoire went down with Marie after the boat exploded."
My necklace glowed a soft purple for a few seconds.

Well, at least the spell works.

"You don't think she found this fire amber?"

"I know she didn't. She thought the map held the answer.
It didn't. That stuff is still lost."

"Really? You solved the map? What did it show?"

"A time imprint. A record of what Angus did and why. I
think he made it after the explosion. Probably for his family,
maybe to clear his name at some point, but the spell that made
it work was lost and it became a mystery."

"How did you get it to work?" Jack narrowed his eyes.

"After the police took you into custody, I translated the
message. Then I found a spell to activate it." I held my breath,
but the teardrop didn't glow. I guess lies by omission didn't
register. "That was a trip, I tell you. Angus' motives were good,
even if his methods weren't. Marie had to be stopped."

Jack nodded, and I noticed his cup was empty. I scooped
it up and stepped to the sink to rinse it. I heard footsteps and
Jack put his hand on my shoulder. I turned, trembling as those
gorgeous blue eyes stared at me. He grinned and I blushed.

Why does he have to be so handsome?

He brushed a stray hair off my cheek. "I'm sorry you got
involved in this. I thought things would turn out differently,
you know." His thumb stroked the edge of my chin. "You had
a smudge of flour. From the bakery, I'm guessing."

I blushed again, this time from embarrassment.

"It seems like forever, that day I came into the bakery. The day before the murder."

I shivered and dropped my gaze.

"I was going to ask you out that day."

"You were?" I stared at him.

"Yeah, until we got interrupted. Then I lost my nerve. I don't think I want to chicken out again." He bent in and kissed me. Our lips met in a moment of heated passion and yearning emotion. The world stopped and every trouble I had melted away.

Then it ended.

Jack stepped back, uncertainty in his eyes. I reached out and took his hand.

"That was…nice. Heck, more than nice, it was amazing."

He laughed. "I've been wanting to do that forever."

"Well, I'm glad you finally acted." Then impulsively I asked, "You want to stay and watch a movie? I'll make popcorn."

"Sounds like fun."

"Great. You find some choices on Netflix while I throw some popcorn in the microwave."

"How about a murder mystery?"

I nearly threw something at him as he walked into the living room.

I heard the TV turn on as I put a bag of microwave popcorn on to heat and took a large bowl out of the cupboard. With all the noise, I almost missed it.

"I can't believe I didn't clue in to what Johnson was up to."

Jack's voice drifted out of the living room, and my necklace glowed a violet colour.

I froze, the bowl poised over the counter, before I plunked it down in shock. Seconds later, Jack stood in the kitchen doorway.

"That was stupid of me. That necklace of yours is some kind of magical lie detector, isn't it?"

I nodded.

"I thought I saw it glow earlier, when you mentioned the grimoire going down with the boat." He moved a step closer. "That's not what happened, is it? You found it."

I wanted to lie and say no, but that was pointless with my own spell ready to rat me out.

"Marie left it behind. It was in her sanctuary, disguised as another book."

"You had it all this time." He chuckled. "What a little liar you are. A good one too. I didn't suspect until tonight."

"Talk about the kettle calling the pot black. You lied about everything."

"Not everything. I do like you." He moved closer and I started looking for an escape route. "What do you want the grimoire for, Bridget? What are you planning?"

That made me angry, maybe because it hit too close to the mark. "I'm not planning anything! I'm trying to rid myself of the mess you and Jillian made. Making sure that book doesn't get in the wrong hands." The necklace didn't glow, so maybe my motives weren't so tainted.

"Then we have that in common."

"Except I never killed anyone!"

"Ah, so you figured that out too, did you?"

"I didn't want to believe it, that you were responsible for all of this. Now I want to know why."

"Does that really matter? Be a good girl and fetch me the grimoire."

"What if I don't?"

He pulled a knife out of his pocket. "Then Hannah gets to find your dead body in a ransacked house. No doubt that will get blamed on Jillian too."

My hand twitched, and I wondered if I could make it to the knife block and grab something to defend myself.

Jack seemed to read my mind. "Don't try, Bridget. I'm stronger than you. It won't end well. And you don't have a wand or handy spells to defend yourself with. That's the only way you would win. Even then, it might be close. I'm a strong witch."

He was right about that, but I might have a trick or two up my sleeves. I had to buy some time.

"Okay. The grimoire is upstairs."

"Show me."

I led him upstairs to the closet and slid the bag with the book off the shelf. I also tucked my little magical booby trap inside the bag without Jack seeing. Then I removed my necklace and dropped it. No point giving him another advantage.

He waved the knife at me. "Take it downstairs. Back to the kitchen. I don't trust that you don't have a wand stashed up here." He grabbed my arm and shoved me to the door. I stumbled out into the hallway and hustled back downstairs. Jack kept pace, making sure I didn't bolt. We ended up sitting across from each other at the kitchen table.

"Show me the grimoire."

I scowled at him, and pulled the book out of the bag, pushing the sack aside, leaving it conveniently located.

"What is this? What are you trying to pull? I said I wanted the grimoire!" He thrust the knife at my face, inches from my eyes.

"That is the grimoire! I told you Marie disguised it."

Jack relaxed, pulling the knife back. "And you kept the disguise. Clever girl. How do you remove it? Show me."

I placed a hand on the grimoire, looked Jack in the eyes and said, "No. Not until you tell me everything. What have you been up to, and why did you kill Johnson?"

Jack smiled, that grin not looking so attractive anymore. "I could probably figure out how to break the disguise myself, you know. I don't need you."

"Maybe. Marie's magic is strong, though, and I used a specialized spell to crack it. You might be able to hit on something similar, but it'll take a while. Plus, are you knowledgeable enough to remove the disguise permanently?" I smirked as my last remark hit home. "I can do that for you."

Not that I will, you murderous jerk.

Jack sat back in his chair. "Fine, but then you unlock the grimoire or else." He waggled his knife. "I first became suspicious of Johnson when he started sniffing around about the map. He said he represented a buyer, someone who collected items related to Marie LeBlanc. I didn't believe him. I believed he was after the grimoire."

Jack sighed. "All my life I heard stories about Angus, George, and Marie, how the map led to a treasure, how it was our legacy. I was convinced it led to Marie's grimoire. That book I lent you. That wasn't my grandfather's. I bought it. I recently figured out the Theban alphabet connection; I hadn't started researching yet when you came along."

I scowled. "So, you figured you'd use the expert and save yourself the trouble?"

"Something like that. Until the police interfered."

"Why did the police pick you up?"

"They found out about my involvement with Johnson. That we had some disagreements. Even before that day at the bakery."

"How did you go from suspecting Johnson of looking for the grimoire to hiring him?"

"Once I figured he was up to no good, I followed him. It wasn't hard; he wasn't very bright. I caught him breaking into your bakery at night. That confirmed everything. He was looking for Marie's hidden room and the grimoire."

"How long were the break-ins happening?" Inside, I fumed.

"About a month. Maybe more." Jack shrugged. "I confronted Johnson about what he was doing, and he admitted he was working for a coven member. He wouldn't say who, just that she wanted anything and everything related to Marie LeBlanc. Including locating her sanctuary. So, I made a deal of my own. Paid him to come to me first if he found anything. Said we sell anything valuable and split the money."

"Why? That doesn't make any sense."

"Of course it does. Keep your friends close, and your enemies closer. Remember, this was before I figured out how to decipher the map." Jack smirked. "Plus, why do all the work yourself, when a lackey can do it?"

"Well, aren't you clever." I wanted to wipe that smirk off his face. It made me sick to think I once considered that smile attractive.

"I was. My plan was to keep him on the hook long enough to figure out who the other player was. I was close too, before that greedy man decided to double-cross all his partners." Jack leaned forward. "I never set out to kill him. He forced my hand."

"How?"

"I never trusted him, so I set up a magical surveillance system in his house. He was talking to people about the possibility of selling some big magical item on the black market, asking about prices. And he went to the library, looking at old blueprints of the bakery, a fact he never mentioned to me. I knew he had figured something out, though what I don't know; I studied those plans years ago and never found anything."

Jack grabbed my hand, the hilt of the knife rubbing my knuckles. "Don't you see, Johnson screwed me over, like George and Marie did to Angus. I couldn't let him find the grimoire and sell it. I wasn't going to let him win." He let go of me and sat back. "No, I wasn't going to let him win. So I didn't."

"By murdering him?"

Jack shrugged. "Seemed like the best option. Stopped him from interfering and shut his mouth permanently. Besides, I had another plan. I didn't need him anymore."

"Another plan? What?"

"You."

My stomach churned. "What do you mean?"

"Hannah's little matchmaking. It dawned on me: date you and I could get close enough to copy your keys. Have free access to the bakery. And I did like you, so…"

I wanted to throw up.

"Why kill him in my bakery?"

"That was bad luck. I knew he was planning another break-in that night, but I dosed the flask with cyanide earlier in the day. I assumed he'd drink from it before breaking in; he nursed it like it was a baby bottle."

"Why cyanide? Why not shoot him or something?"

"Shooting is too messy. Plus, I wanted to get creative. It's amazing what a few fruit pits and a spell can do. Just rotten luck he refrained from indulging until he was in the bakery. I guess things worked out in the end, though."

A satisfied look crossed his face. I repressed a shudder.

"This was about getting even, eliminating a rival? A race to get to the grimoire first?" Anger started creeping up. "For what, your ego? Family pride?"

"No. I eliminated a threat, like Angus did. And I needed time. To figure out what Johnson knew, to find Marie's sanctuary, to decipher the map. Even after everything, I ran out of time and you beat me to it." He shook his head. "Honestly, I never wanted to get you involved."

"No, you wanted to use me." I glared. "It probably would have worked too. You want to know the kicker, even after the murder, I didn't want to be involved. Would have avoided it, except for one thing you didn't count on. Johnson's ghost."

"Yeah, that was a shock. I knew there was a possibility of his ghost, but I never thought he'd go to you. I had to scramble the first time after I realized. Still, I managed to turn that to my advantage. Why do you think I really came here tonight?" He chuckled.

I stared, confused for a moment and then it hit me. He was eavesdropping.

"You used the ghost to spy on me?" This time all my outrage came out. "You were controlling him?"

Jack nodded. "A happy accident of weaving in a tracking spell and an inhibiting spell in with the cyanide. A little precaution in case of ghostly messages; I thought any manifestations might lead me to his first partner. Instead, I heard all your little exchanges and kept tabs on you. It was a bit of a surprise when you summoned him tonight and were asking questions about his second partner. Me."

"And you came over to distract me, allay my suspicions?"

"Something like that. I needed you to focus on Jillian, not me."

"You really are a creep, you know that?"

"I prefer to think of it as pragmatism. Doing what's needed to survive." Jack tapped the knife blade on the table. "Now it's your turn. Unmask the grimoire."

"I'll need a few things. Candles, crystals and rune stones, plus I have to set up a conjuring circle."

"Better get to it, then. I'm running out of patience. Where do you store everything?"

"I should have everything I need in the kitchen."

I knew I did, because I stuffed everything in a cupboard after the last time. I rose, sliding my hand across the table as I did. It would only take a moment to grab the hex bag…

Then a pounding on the front door startled us both.

Chapter 18: Just Desserts

"Who's that? Was Hannah planning to come over?"

"No! I don't know who that is."

Jack snarled, "Why is your house so popular tonight? Ignore it. They'll go away."

But an even more furious round of knocking sounded and a female voice screaming, "I know you're in there!"

"That's Jillian!" I stared at Jack, astonished.

He laughed, stood up abruptly, grabbing my arm and yanking me away from the table. I managed a sideways glance at the bag, now out of reach, before I was propelled out of the kitchen and to the front door.

Jack slid to one side, knife poised to attack, and barked, "Answer it."

I swung open the door and Jillian barged right in, sweeping past both Jack and myself, screaming, "You ruined my life!"

For half a second, I considered bolting out the open door, until Jack slammed it shut and pushed me to one side, grinning at Jillian.

He waved his knife. "Glad you could join us."

Jillian stared for a minute. "What the— I don't know what you're trying to pull, but you picked the wrong woman." She yanked a small gun out of her jacket pocket and pointed it at Jack.

The look on Jack's face nearly made me laugh. He lowered the knife immediately, but didn't drop it.

I decided to roll with this sudden reversal of circumstance. "I didn't ruin your life, Jillian, he did! He's the one who killed Johnson. He's the one that caused all this trouble."

"Wait, what?" Her gun wavered a bit between me and Jack and my skin prickled. "I thought you killed Johnson. That you caught him in the act, wanted to keep Marie's secrets for yourself."

"I didn't even know Marie existed until after he was dead."

"Tell her what else you found." Jack's soft voice entered the discussion. I watched the knife twitch in his hand.

Jillian looked at him. "What do you mean?"

"She found the grimoire."

Jillian snorted. "Oh, that. Big deal. A collection of old spells. Do you know how much magic has advanced since the 1920s? It's a curiosity at best. The only thing of interest in that book is the counterspell. It was Marie's lair I was after, and the map. I needed clues to the fire amber, not some dusty old book."

She turned back to me. "And you're going to help me find it."

I shook my head. "Do you know how dangerous that stuff is? You don't want to mess with it. Besides, I have no clue where Angus hid it."

"Don't believe her." Jack glared at both of us. "She's a liar." He pointed his knife at me.

I snorted, but stepped back. "I hate to break it to you, but we all are."

"Shut up!" Jillian shouted and we both stopped talking. Jack lowered his weapon. "Save your lovers' quarrel for your own time. Where's the fire amber?"

I took a breath. "Why do you want it so badly? Money, control? None of that is worth the harm you could do."

Jillian shot me a look of disgust. "I know what you all think of me, but I don't need more money, and who'd want to control this sorry world? No, I need it to change what happened. To bring him back."

"To bring who back?"

For a minute she looked as if she wanted to tell me off, yet she answered the question, her voice soft and dejected.

"My son. He died. A car hit him." Her voice tightened. "Some drunk. He was only ten."

My throat tightened. "Oh, I'm sorry." I wanted to reach out, but I knew she would reject any sympathy. "You wanted to change that, change events?"

She nodded. "Yes."

"Is that the reason you came here to Easthaven Bay? Did his death set up the chain of events that sent you searching for Marie's secrets?"

Again, she nodded.

"Then the fire amber won't do you any good. That's a paradoxical event. It will create a time loop of failed attempts that will constantly collapse, reset, and recreate itself. Personal cause and effect can't be changed. You change your son's death, and all the ripples change your actions. You won't come to Easthaven Bay. You won't look for the amber or use it. That's why Marie created the counterspell, to undo a paradox."

Jillian turned to me and barked, "Don't you think I know that? It was all in Marie's letter. I know I can fix it, I know I can. I just have to let my past self know what to do to avoid the loop."

"No, Jillian. It won't work. Even Marie couldn't make it work. Let it go."

"You're lying! I can make it work!" In her distress, Jillian let the hand holding her gun drop. Jack surged forward, but he didn't make it far. She smacked him in the face with the butt of the gun. He stumbled back, bleeding. Jillian trained her weapon at his head.

She snarled, "Stupid move. Don't even think about doing that again. And toss the knife. Now!"

Holding his head, Jack challenged her. "What if I don't?"

She laughed. "Then I shoot you and call it self-defence."

His weapon clattered to the floor.

Jillian waved the gun at both of us. "March. Into the living room. I need to think."

She herded us onto the couch and started pacing back and forth. I scooched as far away from Jack as possible trying to figure a way out.

Then it dawned on me.

"You can still get out of this mess, Jillian."

Jillian halted her nervous pacing. "What are you talking about?"

"Yeah," Jack chimed in. "What are you up to?"

"Jillian hasn't done anything criminal, unlike you." I scowled at Jack.

Jack sneered. "What about hiring Johnson? Or aren't break-ins illegal now?"

I shrugged. "Who's to say she knew what he was up to? She hired him in good faith to uncover more about her ancestor, Marie LeBlanc, and be a go-between for the purchase of a map. Isn't that right, Jillian?"

She smiled, catching on. "Yeah, that's right. I had no idea he was a criminal. I'm not the one who killed him."

"You said it yourself, Jack: Johnson wasn't trustworthy. He was double crossing everybody, willing to steal an antique grimoire, sell it and pocket the money."

"He was?" Jillian sounded shocked. "Why that louse!"

Jack was fidgeting now, squirming in his seat. "She's still in trouble with the Council. They'll blackball her for what she's done."

"Maybe not. I mean, there's no proof she was planning on using the grimoire or the fire amber. Why, maybe she unwisely took it upon herself to locate those items for the Council. She said herself she believed I killed Johnson over Marie's secrets. If she thought I was after the grimoire and the amber, it would be her word against the daughter of the great Vivian Redwood. She was protecting the town from me, not knowing we were both innocent."

"Yeah, that's right." Jillian was getting fully immersed now. "I was trying to help."

Jack laughed. "You don't really expect the Council to buy that malarkey, do you?"

"They will if I back up Jillian's story." Jack looked decidedly uncomfortable now. "If I recant my former accusations, explain I was mistaken, the Council will discipline her, and she'll be off the hook."

"You'd do that?" Jillian stared at me.

"Yeah, I will. If you stop this insane plan about the amber. It won't work. All it's done is cause trouble and led to murder."

Jillian bit her lip. Silence dangled between us, but she nodded. I didn't know if she meant it, but I had no choice but to trust her at this point. I eyed my purse, sitting on the coffee table where I plunked it when I came home.

"I'm going to reach for my purse, for my cellphone."

I raised my hand until Jillian barked, "Wait." I froze. "If you double-cross me, I'll make you pay."

"I won't." I eyed Jack. "I just want justice and him in jail."

Jillian nodded. "Okay, fine. Call the cops."

Jack scowled at the both of us, shifting in his seat until Jillian waggled the gun at him.

She smiled. "I can still shoot you."

I grabbed my purse before anyone else objected, pulled out my cell phone and called 911.

The police arrived swiftly and luckily believed the story Jillian and I told; they arrested Jack, and escorted all of us to the nearest police station. Sitting in an interrogation room across from the same officer who interviewed me the day of the murder, I spilled out the truth. Well, most of it.

"Jack confessed to me that he killed Mr. Johnson. I guess my landlord double-crossed him in some underhanded business deal."

"We are aware the two had an arrangement. They weren't as discreet as they believed. Did he disclose any details?"

"Only that they were searching for some 1920s hideout or artifacts they believed were hidden in my bakery. I think it was tall tales and nonsense." I smiled as I lied. "I've never come across any secret anything in that place."

"Yes, Mr. MacNeil has been going on about a woman called Marie LeBlanc and her," the officer looked at his notes, "grimoire. We've called for a psychiatric consultation."

I blinked. They thought Jack was crazy? Well, at least they didn't believe his story.

"Did Mr. MacNeil explain why he killed Mr. Johnson?"

I shrugged. "Not really. I think he didn't trust him or something."

"A quarrel among thieves?"

I said nothing, only shrugged again.

"Now please explain Ms. Burke's involvement and how she ended up at your house with a gun."

"That was a coincidence." I hoped Jillian stuck to our story. "I don't know whether Ms. Burke was an official suspect in the murder, only that rumours were flying around town that she was guilty. She thought I was the murderer and foolishly came over to confront me, make me confess or something to clear her name."

"With a gun?"

"I think that was for self-protection. I mean, she thought I was a killer. And it was a good thing she did. She probably saved my life when she stumbled into Jack taking me hostage."

"About that." The officer tapped his notebook with a pen. "Why do you think Mr. MacNeil threatened you?"

"He made a slip of the tongue. Said something suspicious and I challenged him. Stupid, I know. Then he confessed. Maybe he wanted to brag or something." No need to tell them I blackmailed that confession out of him. "I'm glad Jillian showed up when she did, or who knows what would have happened."

"Yes, it seems you were very lucky." The officer's eyes narrowed, and for a minute I wondered if he suspected I wasn't telling the whole truth. "Also lucky for you, Mr. MacNeil repeated his confession to us. And that Ms. Burke backed up your story. We have some loose ends to tie up, but you'll be free to go soon."

And with that, the officer closed his notebook and left.

I closed my eyes and sighed. It was over.

Chapter 19: Stray Crumbs

"I can't believe I missed all the excitement!" Hannah dropped by the next day, demanding all the details. I decided to leave the bakery in the hands of my assistants for a couple of days to avoid endless repetitions of the story, but I couldn't duck Hannah, even if we had been at odds. I gave her all the juicy details over coffee.

"It's wild that Jack was actually the killer. I mean, I had my doubts about Jillian and suspicions he wasn't telling us everything, still it's incredible that he murdered Mr. Johnson. He seemed so nice."

"Yeah. There was way more to Jack than we realized. You should have seen him last night, Hannah. He was a different person. Obsessed and driven. The only thing that mattered was the grimoire. It was scary."

"Speaking of the grimoire, what are you planning to do with it?" Hannah traced a finger around the rim of her cup.

"I'm turning it over to the Council. There's a meeting tonight to review my and Jillian's actions, and I'm taking the grimoire with me." Part of me didn't like it but the decision was made. I wasn't changing my mind. "I've already told them it exists, so no going back."

"Good." Hannah relaxed. "That thing is more trouble than it is worth."

"It does seem to be a magnet for trouble alright. And I don't want to deal with any more problems caused by dead witches."

"Yeah, let the Council handle it." Yet, she stared morosely into her coffee.

"What's bothering you?"

She looked up. "It's, well, we didn't solve the whole mystery, did we?"

"What do you mean? The murderer has been caught and Johnson can rest in peace, we found Marie's hidden sanctuary and her grimoire, and deciphered Angus' map."

"But we didn't locate the fire amber. I was so sure the map revealed the location. What did Angus do with it? Where did he hide it? It bugs me that we didn't figure that out. Did he throw it in the ocean? Bury it in a deep, dark, hole? Maybe he hid it on the boat and it was destroyed in the explosion."

"Well, that's the Council's problem now."

"I guess. I'm bummed we'll probably never know."

Watching her sad face, I relented. "There's no reason we can't try to work out what happened. As purely an intellectual exercise."

She immediately brightened and grinned. "Oh. Of course. Purely as an intellectual exercise. Where do we start?"

"With ice cream and theorizing on the couch." I dished out two large bowls of chocolate fudge and we settled in on the living room sofa binging on chocolate and spitting out ideas.

"So," Hannah began our session, "everyone thought the map showed the way to where Angus hid the fire amber. Why?"

"I think that's what Angus led everyone to believe. Or the family misinterpreted something and that became the family tale. There seemed to be conflicting stories in the MacNeil clan. Jack was convinced the map led to the grimoire."

"Now why was that, I wonder? If the map was a record of events, why wouldn't Angus let his family know that? Why be cryptic about it? Why the confusion? How did the rumour of it leading to treasure start?"

"Good questions. Why be secretive about it at all? My first assumption was he wanted to clear his name, at least to his family, if not the Council. After watching the time imprint, I figured it was his insurance, the one he mentioned to Marie when she threatened to kill him. Yet why keep it after she was dead? George didn't seem to be a threat, so keeping it doesn't make sense."

Hannah nodded. "And another thing that doesn't make sense. After he stole the fire amber, why not turn it over to the Council and let them deal with Marie? Sure, he was a bit of a rogue, but if he handed them Marie LeBlanc on a silver platter, he could have worked out a deal. Yet he chose to hide the amber, murder her, and let himself and his family be tossed out of the coven. Blowing up the boat seems like a big unnecessary risk."

"Murder seems to be the go-to option for the MacNeils." I spooned some ice cream in my mouth as I sorted through Hannah's logic. "Angus' actions are odd. It's like he deliberately made things difficult and convoluted. They all did. That 1920s bunch was paranoid and obsessed with secrets."

"I guess engaging in criminal activity can make you distrustful."

I frowned. "Yeah, Angus was a criminal, wasn't he? Kind of self-centered too, maybe. Remember what he said to Marie? Something about the Council coppers and not wanting to get rubbed out. He seemed more worried about saving his skin than actual repercussions about using the amber."

"What? You think he kept it for himself? Used it?" Hannah clued into what I was thinking, before adding, "How? Wouldn't someone have noticed the magic? Wouldn't there have been repercussions?"

"Depends on how he used it. Making the time imprint didn't raise any flags. And keeping the map makes more sense if he was using the amber for himself. An alibi of sorts if someone got suspicious. Like, 'Sure I have fire amber, but here's why. I was saving the world.'"

"If it's true, that's diabolical. And a rum-running scoundrel double-crossing his partners does fit better than his suddenly growing a conscience."

"It could also mean he murdered Marie and tried to murder George. No witnesses and no rivals."

Hannah's spoon clattered against her bowl. "That's cold-blooded."

I nodded. The MacNeil genetics were dark. "Yeah. Maybe he justified it. Marie was a threat to everyone." I shrugged. "The question is, what did he use the amber for and how has it stayed hidden for so long?"

Hannah sighed. "I guess that's a secret Angus took to the grave."

I swirled my spoon in the last remnants of ice cream. "Did he, though? He knew how dangerous fire amber is, and however much of a scoundrel he was, would he be that irresponsible? Just leave the amber for someone to find?"

"You think he left a clue? Something we missed?"

I nodded. "I keep coming back to the map. Why did everyone believe it led to the fire amber? Even Jillian. Why did everyone think it was important? After all these years?"

"Yeah. That's strange. No one ever challenged him, so Angus wouldn't have needed it. Why attach any importance to it at all?"

"Let's have another look at it." I uncurled from the couch and stood.

Hannah joined me, a surprised look on her face. "You still have it?"

I shrugged as we walked to the kitchen. "We never turned it over to the Council, remember? It wasn't illegal and belonged to the MacNeils. Now, with Jack in jail and none of the other MacNeils showing up to claim it, it is still sitting in a drawer."

"Well, let's look at it, then."

I dug the map out from the drawer where I stuffed it and unrolled it on the counter, holding down the edges with the salt and pepper and a couple of glasses.

"We know the thing's an imprint, and an encoded message, but what else?"

"If there's something else," Hannah amended.

"True. Let's proceed on the assumption there is something we missed. It's not uncommon for witches to use a threefold spellworking."

"Okay, so hide the message, hide the imprint and hide…what?"

"The location of the fire amber?"

"Another message? Or…" She stopped and stared at the map. "A treasure map. Maybe it's that simple. They must have tried that, so it would have to be…" She looked up. "Help me out here. Is it possible to work a triggered revealing spell into an object, something that needs a specific word or phrase to activate it, hidden under layers of other magic? I recall that from advanced magic class, only I can't remember the specifics."

I nodded. "It's not common anymore, but yeah. Most witches use protection spells these days to safeguard secrets."

"Was it more common in Angus' day?"

"Maybe. Are you thinking he disguised an actual map under the hidden message and the time imprint?"

"Yes. Do you know how these keyword reveal spells worked?"

"From what I remember it's a standard revealing spell with a standard trigger spell attached. The trick is figuring out the keyword."

"So, it's trial and error then." Hannah smiled. "Let's do this. Nothing to lose right?"

I nodded and gathered up the candles, crystals and runes we needed for the spell, setting them in place. Then I recited the revealing spell, using the same variant I used for the grimoire.

"Candle, Crystal, and Rune show us what we seek. Candle, Crystal, and Rune, reveal the secrets hidden. Candle, Crystal, and Rune, unveil the invisible."

And nothing happened. Not that I expected anything.

"Now what?" Hannah asked.

"Now we do trial and error." I exhaled and said "Angus MacNeil." Nothing. Guess old Angus didn't have that big an ego.

Hannah tried, "Fire amber." Nothing. And then, "Rum." Still nothing.

For a good hour we tried every word or phrase that came to mind, including some 1920s slang, but the map stayed stubbornly unchanged.

Finally I said, "Let's take a break. It's nearly lunch and I have to meet with the Council afterwards. Hannah nodded and we put everything away, including the map, which I slid back in the drawer.

I came home after facing the Council, drained, and off the hook for my actions. I was surprised they were so lenient, on both myself and Jillian. The grimoire was gone, safely in their hands now. I felt surprisingly relieved. Everything seemed fresher, as if a shadow had been lifted.

"Good riddance, Marie LeBlanc."

A blazing glow lit up one certain drawer.

"What the—" I yanked open the drawer and stared at Angus' map, now showing a very detailed drawing of Easthaven Bay and a small red X. I slowly closed the drawer and called Hannah.

She must have flown over, she arrived so fast. Red-faced and full of excitement, she raced into the kitchen after I let her in, with me at her heels. I pulled out the map and showed her.

"I can't believe we never thought of using her name earlier! It's so obvious."

"Yeah. I guess it was Angus' private joke."

"Where's the stuff located?" She studied the map and then looked at me confused. "That can't be right."

"It's weird, I'll admit, but that building is old enough. The timeline fits, right?"

"Yeah. I think they were even doing renovations the year Marie died, so I guess it fits. Why there, though? Why would Angus hide the fire amber in the clocktower?"

"Maybe another joke? Hide the thing that alters time in a clock? I mean, it's very appropriate. The tick, tick of the clock…" I frowned, a thought forming, mumbling, "The tick, tick of the clock, always in time with fire amber. Could it be possible? Would he even need to touch it if he used it as a scrying spell?"

"Use what? What are you thinking?" Hannah demanded.

"Something outrageous. What if Angus bonded the amber to the clock? Used the clock to amplify it and opened viewing windows through time. He could spy on his neighbours, find out secrets, all sorts of things."

"And use all that information to his advantage. Quietly and efficiently. Would something like that attract magical attention?"

"I think that would depend on how much he used it. Used sparingly probably not, unless someone was looking for time stream fluctuations."

"So how do we retrieve it? The fire amber, I mean?"

I grinned. "Another midnight excursion, I think. With the right spell we should be able to detect it and figure out where it is in the clock. Extracting it will be trickier, so maybe leave that to the experts and the Council, but we can definitely locate it."

"Let's get started then."

I dug out my spellbooks and we settled in to work.

Chapter 20: The Last Bite

"Maybe we should let the Council handle this?" Hannah glanced at me, nerves giving her second thoughts. We were standing in the town square yet again, this time across from the clock tower.

I looked at her. I also felt uneasy. "We can go back if you want. I'm fine with letting them handle it from here. We figured out the location, they can do the retrieval."

Hannah frowned, glancing over her shoulder. "Yeah, I think we're overreaching, but first let's make sure we're right. We can reveal the thing without retrieving it, and then tell the Council. Let them handle it."

"Okay. Probably better to verify and not send them on a wild goose chase."

"We agree then."

I nodded and we scurried across the street and snuck around to the rear of the clock tower. Better to work the spell in a more secluded space and then check for any tell-tale signs of a hiding place. It wasn't much of a building; a rather stubby brick tower with a four faced clock mechanism at the top.

Finding where Angus stashed the amber probably wouldn't take long.

I dug the map out of my pocket and took another look by flashlight to make sure we hadn't missed anything. During our research, we noticed a pendulum drawn on the back of the revealed map, so we suspected that's what Angus bonded the amber to in his original spell.

"Ready." I looked over and Hannah set up the rune circle. I handed her the map and she placed it in the center of the ring, weighed down by a crystal. The spell we concocted used the map as the anchor point for a modified scrying spell.

I pulled the written spell out of my pocket along with a pendulum bob. With any luck, one pendulum would call to the other.

I took a breath, swung the bob in a circular motion over the map, and recited, "From the past, reveal the spell, within the workings of the bell. The tick of clock and weave of time, the magic bonding of the chime. We seek the truth, we seek the spell, bring it forth from where it dwells."

Hannah and I held our breath as nothing happened for a few seconds, and then the clock tower lit up like fireworks and a Christmas tree rolled into one, bursting with a sparking orange radiance that shot up into the sky. We scrambled backward, flummoxed.

Hannah shrieked, "That wasn't supposed to happen! We are so screwed."

Then, as quickly as it lit up, the light died down, leaving only one gleaming item floating above the tower.

I sucked in my breath. "Is that what I think it is?"

Hannah whispered, "What did we do wrong? The Council is going to kill us."

As we watched, the fire amber, the same piece we saw in Marie's hands, drifted downward to land on Angus' map, which promptly burst into flames.

"Oh crap!" I stomped the flames out with my foot, but the map was ashes. I grabbed up the amber, which surprisingly wasn't hot, and stuffed it in a pocket.

"Come on, let's get our stuff and get out of here before someone comes."

Hannah and I hastily retrieved our spell ingredients and fled; she returned to her home and I went back to my house. Safely inside, I rolled the amber in a dishcloth and crammed it in the drawer where I had stored the map.

I hope the MacNeils don't come looking for their map.

Tomorrow, I'd take that thing to the Council. For now, I headed to bed.

With another emergency Council meeting called, I headed there in the morning with the fire amber tucked into my purse, and the mental note to bake a couple of batches of brownies for the Council members. I had tested their patience enough, and some sweet treat gift baskets might mend a few fences.

When I arrived at the community centre, Jillian was standing outside the entrance. I slowed my pace, finally stopping in front of her, giving a slight smile. Why was she here? Did she know? Was she going to steal the fire amber? My grip tightened on my purse.

"Jillian. Are you here to meet with the Council, too?"

"No. I'm here to see you. I needed to tell you something."

I braced myself. "What?"

"I wanted you to know. I'm taking your advice, healing from my son's death the old-fashioned way, with time and counselling. No more magical solutions or trying to alter events."

I was surprised, but kind of proud of Jillian. Maybe she wasn't such a prick after all.

"So you can stop gripping your bag like I was a mugger. I'm not going to steal the fire amber."

Then again, maybe she hadn't changed.

"And don't think this makes us friends. I still can't stand you." She stalked off without another word.

Definitely still a prick.

I shrugged and went inside to face the ire of the Council.

Five members glared at me from the table as I placed the fire amber in front of them and explained what happened. The most senior member, Mr. Landry, cleared his throat.

"It seems you don't learn lessons well, Miss Redwood. What did we tell you about amateur sleuthing? After all the trouble you stumbled into, you went looking for more? Didn't you think we were investigating the whereabouts of the fire amber? Do you think we are incompetent?"

"No, sir, I don't—"

He didn't let me finish.

"I don't know how the covens in Ontario handle things, but here we like people to follow procedures. Do you know how egregious a violation this is? Recovering dangerous artifacts is the job for our retrieval teams, not you or Miss Murphy."

"Yes, sir," I hesitated, but this time he let me explain. "It was never our intention to recover the amber. That was an accident. We only wanted to confirm the location before reporting our findings to the Council. Unfortunately, our locator spell had unforeseen side effects and the amber came to us."

"I see." He cleared his throat. "And why didn't you come to us with your theories instead of confirming them first?"

"We originally thought we were wrong. When we stumbled into the truth, I suppose we were caught in the adventure of it. You have our sincere apologies."

"Thank you for that, at least you seem contrite." Landry leaned back and crossed his arms. "Now, we come to the question of what to do with you. Frankly, we were of a mind to punish this transgression harshly, yet we don't want to discourage initiative in our witches, especially ones of your lineage. So, we weighed those factors, and given the positive end result, we decided to be lenient and overlook your bad judgement. However, this had best be the last time you get 'caught in the adventure'. I hope I make myself clear?"

"Yes, sir." I ducked my head, relieved. Being Vivian Redwood's daughter came in handy this time.

"Then this meeting is over."

I thanked them and hastily left.

Two weeks later, I drove to the prison where Jack was housed. I arranged the visit because I needed closure, so here I was, sitting in the visitor area, waiting for a man who lied to me and probably would have killed me.

Yet I had something to say.

They brought Jack out in handcuffs, dressed in orange sweatpants and a short-sleeved shirt, grinning that same arrogant smirk of his. Only it wasn't so attractive anymore. He still made my heart race, but not because I liked him. This time it was with anger.

He slid into the seat opposite me. "So, you couldn't stay away. Should I be flattered?"

"No. I came to let you know some things we found out after you got arrested." I leaned in slightly. "About Angus."

That got Jack's attention and he dropped the smarmy attitude, his expression now dark. "What?"

I smiled. "You admired him, didn't you? Thought he was caught in an impossible situation and went to extreme measures to protect his family, the town? That's how you justified your own actions."

Jack scowled. I could see in his eyes I struck a nerve, and I was right.

"Well, dear old Angus wasn't the tarnished saint you believed. He was a killer like you."

I watched Jack curl his fingers into fists, his anger barely contained.

I took a breath, choosing my words carefully. "You know that thing he stole? Well, I found it, figured out what happened, and why. Angus' motives for the theft were a bit different than we assumed. He used it, Jack, rigged it so he would always have an advantage. That's how the MacNeil family went from lowly rumrunners and scoundrels to pillars of the community. Angus stole, cheated, and murdered his way to the top. He was no better than Marie. Maybe worse."

Jack hissed. "You're lying."

I shook my head. "Check out my story. I'm sure you still have contacts in the Council that can verify what I said."

"So you came here to gloat?"

"No. I'm here to show you what kind of man you are, that none of your actions were noble, or for the greater good. You carried on a twisted legacy of your family and you are exactly where you deserve to be."

I rose and nodded to the guard, who escorted a fuming Jack back to his cell.

With a sense of satisfaction, I headed home; I was in the mood to return to a normal routine, do some baking, have some fun.

Maybe I'd invite Hannah for a girl's night.

Maybe I'd even make some fudge.

Maple Fudge Recipe

Want to make your own to-die-for Maple Fudge?

Check out this classic recipe on the Canadian Living
Magazine website.

Maple Fudge

https://www.canadianliving.com/food/baking-and-desserts/
recipe/maple-fudge-2

THANK YOU for reading this story and I hope you enjoyed it. Also, please consider taking the time to leave an honest review. Authors appreciate reader feedback. If you like to know more about me or my books, please drop me a line at my website.

Be Afraid of the Dark.
https://afstewart.ca/

COMING SOON IN THE SERIES

Bewitched Butter Tarts and Burglary
Necromancy and Nanaimo Bars

You can check out the series book page.
https://afstewart.ca/sweet-spells-mysteries/

A. F. STEWART was born and raised in Nova Scotia, Canada, and still calls it home. The youngest in a family of seven children, she is a steadfast and proud sci-fi and fantasy geek with an overly creative mind and an active imagination. She favours the dark and deadly when writing—her genres of choice being dark fantasy and horror—but she has ventured into the light occasionally. As an indie author, she's published novels, novellas and story collections, with a few side trips into poetry.

Books by A. F. Stewart

Cozy Steampunk Paranormal

Heyward and Andersen, Consulting Detectives Series
The Ghostly Tower: A Heyward and Andersen Mystery
Shadow in Scarlet: A Heyward and Andersen Mystery
The Headless Corpse: A Heyward and Andersen Mystery
Rivalry and Steam Monsters: A Heyward and Andersen Mystery

Horror

Entangled Nightmares Series
Fairy Tales and Nightmares: Nine Fairy Tale Retellings
Visions and Nightmares: Ten Stories of Dark Fantasy and Horror

Killers and Demons Series
Killers and Demons
Killers and Demons II: They Return

Dark Epic Fantasy

Saga of the Outer Islands Series
Ghosts of the Sea Moon
Souls of the Dark Sea
Renegades of the Lost Sea

Multi-Author Anthologies

Realms of Horror (Genre Writers of Atlantic Canada Book 2)
Realms of Fantasy (Genre Writers of Atlantic Canada Book 1)
Fairy Tales Punk'd 2
Fairy Tales Punk'd
Cogs, Crowns, and Carriages
Hell's Empire: Tales of the Incursion
Abandon: 13 Tales of Impulse, Betrayal, Surrender, and Withdrawal
A Twist of Fate: A Collection of 11 Twisted Fairy Tales
Beyond the Wail
Legends and Lore
Mechanized Masterpieces
Christmas Lites Series (Books III-IX)